T0287625

THE LOST DIARIES
OF
NIGEL MOLESWORTH

Geoffrey Willans

(Photograph courtesy of Robin Gilbert)

THE LOST DIARIES
of
NIGEL MOLESWORTH

by

Geoffrey Willans

with illustrations by Uli Meyer
(with apologies to Ronald Searle)

a foreword by GYLES BRANDRETH

and an introduction by
ROBERT J. KIRKPATRICK

This edition published in 2022
by Korero Press Ltd
www.koreropress.com

ISBN: 9781912740161

A CIP catalogue record for this book is available from the British Library.

Printed in China

Well over half a century ago, I used to attain a sudden unwonted popularity among my schoolfellows when I received my copy of the latest Molesworth publication before it reached the shops. I also remember my long-suffering Uncle Geoff (or Unkle Goeff, as it is spelt in my signed copy of *Whizz for Atomms*) generously signing his name fifty times on a sheet of paper divided into rectangular boxes, so that I could use them as swops for my autograph collection. Now, more than sixty years later, Geoffrey Willans' star is still justly in the ascendant. In 2018, Molesworth graced the front cover of *The Oldie*, advertising a fine tribute by Michael Barber within, and, only last year, Geoffrey Willans' achievement was honoured by his home city of Gloucester with a plaque on 19 Alexandra Road, where he grew up. Now we have The Lost Diaries. I had read one or two of them in *The Pick of Punch* and was delighted to hear that the full collection was to be published in a single volume. I congratulate Robert Kirkpatrick on bringing his excellent project to completion.

ROBIN GILBERT

The novelist Simon Raven (a great fan of Molesworth), who was at school during World War Two, used to say that his teachers encouraged him to regard the war as "an unpleasant interlude" that should not deter him from mastering Latin and Greek or striving to get his Cricket colours. I was reminded of this by a letter that arrived at *Punch* in May 1940, as Nazi panzers swept towards the Channel. "Dear Mr *Punch*," it began, "Please do not let Molesworth 1 die, he makes tears course the cheeks of this large and active family. For once one forgets Events." How chuffed Willans must have been to read this!

MICHAEL BARBER

Nigel Molesworth was one of the earliest cultural influences on my life. I read him first in the 1950s and in subsequent decades have rarely come across better analyses of the British educational system, indeed of many aspects of the British character, than his. However, at that time, I had no idea that Molesworth's wit and wisdom were going strong as early as 1939. The re-emergence of the work of his early years is long overdue. Some sixty years after I first read *Down With Skool!* it is fascinating for me to discover, through Robert Kirkpatrick's diligent research, how Nigel's highly original outlook on life and language placed him into the pantheon of iconoclastic philosophers even before he took the post-war literary world by storm.

TIM RICE

It is interesting to see the revival of my father's early Molesworth diaries, and I am sure he and my mother would have been proud. My father was a great exponent of the boarding school system. Molesworth's observations are an iconic insight as to how to beat the system and get by. Thank you Robert for keeping the heritage of the character alive.

G.M. WILLANS

Now that you've finished this, can you please get round to cleaning the oven?

CHRISTINE KIRKPATRICK

ACKNOWLEDGEMENTS

FIRSTLY, THANKS ARE DUE to Lou Burnard, via whose blog I was prompted, in 2010, to begin a quest to get these diaries republished. Sorry it took so long.

Secondly, thanks are due to Wendy Cope, for putting me in touch with Geoffrey Willans's nephew, Robin Gilbert.

More importantly, huge thanks are due to Robin Gilbert himself, for providing a great deal of background and supplementary information on Geoffrey Willans's life.

Similar extensive thanks are due to Michael Willans and, in particular, his partner Bente Fladmark, for filling in many remaining gaps, in particular concerning Geoffrey Willans's war career.

Huge thanks also to Uli Meyer, the man behind *The Animated Molesworth*, for his sublime illustrations.

Thanks also to Emily Walhout, at the Houghton Library, Harvard University, for answering my questions about the original typescript of *Down with Skool!*, which the Library acquired in late 2019.

Thanks should also be offered to various noble, brave, fearless idiots on Twitter, Facebook and other social media platforms who have kept the Molesworth legend alive.

Finally, thanks are due to Gyles Brandreth, for kindly writing the Foreword, Sir Tim Rice and Michael Barber.

CONTENTS

FOREWORD

Gyles Brandreth

MOLESWORTH. The name alone does the trick.

Say "Molesworth", and for me, instantly, a complete character and a whole world are conjured up. At once I can visualise the genius illustrations of the master of the spiky, spidery line, Ronald Searle, and the unique way with words – and spelling and capitalisation and schoolboy slang – of Geoffrey Willans, the remarkable man who created Nigel Molesworth, "the curse of St. Custard's", "the goriller of 3B".

Nigel Molesworth first appeared in the weekly humorous magazine *Punch* in 1939. I did not discover him until 1959, when, aged eleven, I was sent away to a boarding prep school in Kent and given a copy of the first Molesworth book, *Down with Skool!* as a taste of things to come.

At its worst, my prep school was not unlike St. Custard's. Our headmaster was called STOCKS, but happily he was a gentle man who did not believe in corporal punishment, quite unlike the Headmaster GRIMES. We definitely had the equivalent of Sigismund Arbuthnot, the mad maths master, though at my school he taught French. When I arrived our Head Boy was exactly like Grabber, "captane of everything", especially "foopball", and "winer of the mrs joyful prize for rafia work". (We did a lot of raffia work in the art class at my school, where I seem to remember the teacher was a small, round, elderly lady called Miss Loewen.) Alarmingly, in retrospect, I realise that if I was like any of the characters in the world of St. Custard's it was probably Basil Fotherington-Tomas. I did not have blond curls, nor did I skip around the school grounds saying "Hullo clouds, hullo sky", but I was undoubtedly a ghastly goody-goody, a wet and a weed.

Until I discovered St. Custard's, my favourite fictional school was Greyfriars, the school created by Frank Richards for *The Magnet* at the beginning of the 20th century and brought to a new audience through *Billy Bunter of Greyfriars School* on television in the 1950s. But Greyfriars and Billy Bunter provided what was essentially children's entertainment. There was something much more grown-up, sophisticated and anarchic in the humour of Geoffrey Willans, who, as a boy, was sent to a preparatory school in Cheltenham and then to Blundell's School in Tiverton, Devon, and later became a schoolmaster. This explains why his portrait of school life is so unnervingly accurate – and yet fundamentally affectionate.

Willans died young, aged only 47, but during his lifetime he was a man of energy and enthusiasms. He was a keen amateur botanist, and it has been said that he had his own key to Kew Gardens. During the war he served in the Royal Navy and maintained his interest in naval affairs. He was a busy writer, publishing two novels before the war and several later books.

But he will be remembered above all, and rightly, for the books *Down with Skool!* (1953), *How to be Topp* (1954), *Wizz for Atomms* (1956) and *Back in the Jug Agane* (1959), collected together in *The Compleet Molesworth*, and the book you are holding in your hand right now: *The Lost Diaries of Nigel Molesworth*. Geoffrey Willans wrote just 20 accounts of Nigel Molesworth's life for *Punch*. Thanks to Robert J. Kirkpatrick, author of *The Encyclopaedia of Boys' School Stories* and other books, and with the blessing of Willans's son, Michael, they are being published here in one volume for the first time. Enjoy! You are in for a treat…

INTRODUCTION

> 6 May. Arrived back at school. Started to cry and went into jim to wear it off. Ragged in jim but was stoped by Mr Trimp (headmaster) and recived conduc mark chiz. Rember have some cigs in plabox and endevore to remove them but Mr Oates (geog) sees me and says what have you got there, nothing sir honestly, I say you can see if you want to sir. He say I trust you molesworth but he follow me when I go out chiz. Will have to wait. Went on raging and mucked about and after tea went and had reeding Mr Trimp read Dr syn. Quite a good book every body gets murded. Mr Trimp says it will be fine tomow.
>
> 7 May. It rained.

So began Nigel Molesworth's debut as a man of letters, in the magazine *Punch* on 9 August 1939.

Most people familiar with Molesworth, who was created by the author Geoffrey Willans, know of him through the four books published in the 1950s – *Down with Skool!*, *How to be Topp*, *Whizz for Atomms* and *Back in the Jug Agane*, all with illustrations by Ronald Searle – or via the omnibus volume *The Compleet Molesworth*.

Not so widely known are the Molesworth diaries that appeared in 20 issues of *Punch* between August 1939 and December 1942. Although Molesworth appears fully formed, with his terrible spelling and cynical view of life, the diaries are substantially different from the later books, both in format and setting.

Willans created Molesworth[1] in 1936, although it took three years for him to appear in print. Writing in the *Young Elizabethan*, a monthly children's magazine published by Collins, in April 1957, Willans noted that the first Molesworth book, presumably based on the diaries, "was to have been produced during the war illustrated by a very brilliant *Punch* artist, called 'Pont'". However, nothing came of this, as "Pont" (actually Graham Laidler, born in 1908) died of poliomyelitis in November 1940.

The Molesworth diaries are usually overlooked in discussions of Molesworth and his creator, presumably because they have never (until now) been republished (although a handful of the diaries have appeared in compilations of *Punch* material). It is also clear that some critics have never read the diaries, which has led to a degree of confusion over the origins of the later Molesworth books. In a rather dismissive essay in *The London Review of Books* (17 February 2000), to mark the re-issue of *The Compleet Molesworth* as a Penguin Classic, Thomas Jones wrote of Molesworth:

> His diaries… originally appeared in *Punch*, as a kind of sequel about a boys' school to Searle's St. Trinian's drawings. They were published in book form as *Down with Skool!* (1953), *How to be Topp* (1954)…

Similarly, Andrew Collins wrote in his 2004 memoir *Where Did It All Go Right?* that

---

1 It is believed that the name Molesworth came from RAF Molesworth in Cambridgeshire, which Willans often passed in the family car when he was a child, and not from the Victorian writer of children's books, Mrs Molesworth (or, indeed, anyone else with the same name).

> *Down with Skool!* was one of four Molesworth books, first published back in the Fifties, collected from *Punch* magazine, not that I was aware of their vintage or genesis.

Two years later Neil Cornwell, in his book *The Absurd in Literature*, refers to "the Molesworth books of Geoffrey Willans and Ronald Searle (first appearing as The Diaries of Molesworth in *Punch* in the early 1950s…)." In 2012, Bruce Ware Allen, in his online *A History Blog*, wrote,

> As early as 1939, Willans had tossed off a few bits and pieces about a precocious and suspicious schoolboy named the Terror of St. Custards.

The most egregious mistake appeared in the magazine *Variety* in February 2020, when Christopher Vourlais wrote (in an article referring to a forthcoming animated film of Molesworth) that Molesworth "was first drawn by Ronald Searle for his *Punch* magazine strip…".

This is all quite wrong. The books consisted of entirely new material, and bear no relation to the diaries – the Second World War was an ever-present theme throughout the diaries, and irrelevant to the books; the diaries were a straightforward record of events and Molesworth's thoughts; and while the books are full of Molesworth's philosophy and examples of his vivid imagination, these are largely absent from the diaries.

It should also be noted that while Ronald Searle's first St. Trinian's cartoon had been published in 1941 (in the magazine *Lilliput*), all the subsequent cartoons were published from 1946 onwards, just over three years after Willans's last Molesworth diary. So the diaries were certainly not a sequel to the St. Trinian's cartoons. Furthermore, the pieces published from 1939 onwards were not, as shown later, set at St. Custard's (and Molesworth actually called himself "The Curse of St. Custards", as any fule kno). And, of course, Ronald Searle never contributed Molesworth drawings to *Punch*.[2]

THE AUTHOR

Geoffrey Willans was the second of three children born to George Herbert Willans and his wife Alice Elizabeth, née Weiss. George, born in Wrexham, Wales, in 1880, was working on the Ottoman (Aidin) Railway as an Assistant Locomotive Carriage and Wagon Superintendent, having begun his working life in 1895 as an apprentice to his father with the Wrexham, Mold and Connah's Quay Railway, and later becoming an Inspector of Materials for the Great Central Railway in Gorton, Lancashire. He moved to Smyrna (then in Greece but now known as Izmir, in Turkey) in 1905, where he met Alice Elizabeth Weiss (known as Biddy), born in Bristol in 1883 and then working as a governess for a wealthy Greek family. They returned briefly to England to marry in Wallsend, Northumberland, on 6 August 1908.

After a further five years in Smyrna, the couple settled in Gloucester in 1913, initially at 22 Heathville Road and later, from 1918 onwards, at 19 Alexandra Road. George worked as a freelance inspecting engineer and a designer of railway rolling stock. He died on 2 January 1947, with Biddy dying on 17 February 1978.

---

2 It is also worth noting that the Wikipedia page on Willans refers to him, quite erroneously, as "the co-creator, with Ronald Searle, of Nigel Molesworth...".

Their three children were George Alec, born on 12 May 1909 in Smyrna (he became a solicitor, and died on 3 May 1973); Geoffrey; and Joyce, born on 20 January 1914 in Gloucester – in 1937 she married Richard Greynvile Gilbert, then a classics master at Bedford School but soon to move to Stowe as Head of English; she died in Oxford on 20 January 1993 (her 79th birthday).

Geoffrey Willans (christened Herbert Geoffrey Willans) was born on 4 February 1911 in Smyrna and, after his parents' return to England was educated at Glyngarth Preparatory School in Cheltenham, Gloucestershire, between 1918 and 1924, and then at Blundell's School in Tiverton, Devon, leaving in 1929.

What Willans did immediately after leaving Blundell's is not known. On the back cover of the dustwrapper of his novel *The Whistling Arrow*, published in 1957, he is quoted as saying, "I taught in a succession of very odd places until rescued by the war when I joined the Navy in 1940." Not all the schools he taught at have been identified, but it is strongly believed that he taught at Sutherland House, a prep school in Windlesham, Surrey, in around 1930/1931. This was run by Oswald Hall Bradnack, a rather fierce man who had taken over his father's school, then in Folkestone, Kent, and moved it to Windlesham in 1905, taking over and renaming an existing prep school, Woodcote House. The school's fortunes began to plummet in the late 1920s, and it was taken over by H.D.L. Paterson in 1931, who changed its name back to Woodcote House.

Willans subsequently became an assistant master at Carn Brea Preparatory School, Bromley, Kent (founded in 1923 and closed in around 1973). How long he taught there is not known, although it is thought he left some time before 1936.

He later taught at Woodcote House, joining in the summer term of 1937 and leaving in 1939 or early 1940. He did not, as some sources say, return to Blundell's to teach.

In the meantime, he had begun a second career as a journalist and author, publishing two humorous novels, *Shallow Dive* in 1934 and *Romantic Manner* in 1936, and also contributing to magazines including *Punch* and, later, *Lilliput*. At the same time he was an active sailor, and after an unsuccessful attempt to join the Royal Navy in 1938, he joined the Royal Naval Volunteer Reserve as a Probationary Temporary Lieutenant (later becoming a Lieutenant) in May 1940. He spent several weeks at HMS King Alfred, a shore-based training establishment at Hove, Sussex, and then three weeks on anti-submarine training at Portland, Dorset. He subsequently joined the corvette HMS Peony in Belfast, serving as a Gunnery Officer (on the strength of a short course he had undertaken at HMS Excellent on Whale Island, Portsmouth), initially escorting convoys in the Atlantic and then in the Mediterranean, sailing to Gibraltar, Malta, Crete, Port Said, Alexandria and Tobruk. (Many of the Molesworth diaries were written in his cabin.) In 1941 he was transferred to the aircraft carrier HMS Formidable, which sailed from Alexandria, via the Red Sea and Cape Town, to America for repairs. He subsequently published an account of his experiences in *One Eye on the Clock* in 1943.

Immediately prior to joining HMS Peony, on 9 November 1940, he had married Pamela Wyndham Gibbes at St. Mary Abbots Church, Kensington, London. Pamela, born on 11 July 1912, was the daughter of Lewes Nicholas Gibbes, a doctor, and his wife Mignonette, née Middlemass. Geoffrey and Pamela went on to have two sons – Nicholas Geoffrey, born on 14 March 1943 (died on 24 August 2002), and George Michael, born on 20 February 1947.

Willans went on to serve at two shore-based naval establishments, HMS Victory in Portsmouth and HMS Dundonald at Gailes on Scotland's Firth of Clyde, in 1942 and early 1943. In March 1943 he joined the troopship The Duchess of Bedford and sailed to Suez, after which he was transferred to the Reina del Pacifico (a Pacific Steam Navigation Company passenger ship being used as a troopship) and in July 1943 was involved in Operation Husky, the invasion of Sicily. He subsequently spent some time in Malta and Alexandria before being shipped to Bombay in September 1943.

In February 1944 Willans moved to Chittagong (then in Bengal) and in March he took part in Operation Screwdriver, a raid against the Japanese in Burma. He then returned to Bombay, and in June 1944 was transferred to Ceylon (Sri Lanka), working at the Commander-in-Chief's Headquarters in Colombo and becoming involved in the bombardment of Japanese positions around Sebang, Sumatra. In October 1944 he was moved to the Naval Headquarters at Trincomalee, Ceylon, where he stayed until April 1945.

A second account of his exploits remains unpublished, although a comic novel which drew on his experiences, *Admiral on Horseback*, was published in 1954. The same year also saw the publication of *The Wit of Winston Churchill*, co-edited with Charles Roetter and illustrated by the cartoonist "Vicky" (Victor Weisz).

Having left the RNVR, Willans had planned on becoming a full-time freelance writer, but in December 1945 he realised that he needed to get a job and so began working for Reuters, before joining the BBC European Service in June 1946. He also continued contributing to various magazines (including *Britannia and Eve, The Sphere* and *Blackwood's Magazine*). In 1947 he moved his family from 92 Kensington Church Street, Kensington, London (the Gibbes family home) to Mill End House, Clavering, Essex (which he had bought in 1946 and restored). He continued working in London, commuting from Audley End station.

In 1956 Willans published *Fasten Your Lapstraps!*, a comic guide to intercontinental air travel, and the novel *Crisis Cottage*. These were followed a year later by *My Uncle Harry*, a fictional portrait of an eccentric Edwardian gentleman and the world of London clubs; the novel *The Whistling Arrow*, about the people who manufacture and fly aircraft; and a biography of actor Peter Ustinov.

In early 1958 he fulfilled his dream and became a freelance writer. His last work, apart from the fourth Molesworth book, was the humorous *The Dog's Ear Book*, in collaboration with Ronald Searle, and the screenplay, written in conjunction with the film director Frank Launder, of *The Bridal Path* (based on the novel of the same name by Nigel Tranter), which was released in 1959.

Willans died suddenly, of a heart attack, at the London Hospital, Shoreditch, on 6 August 1958. He left an estate valued at £3,027 15s 8d (net value £2,042 6s 9d – around £43,000 in today's terms). His wife died on 20 February 1979 at Homestalls, Punnets Town, East Sussex, the family home she had bought after she moved from Clavering.

Sadly, the last resting place of Geoffrey Willans is not known – indeed, it is not known if he was buried or cremated.

Ronald Searle said that Willans was "shortish, dapper – a careful dresser. Very accessible, with a splendidly broad smile.

Slightly clownlike… But there was nothing clownish about him. Entirely professional."[3] He added that he "must have been a jolly nice schoolmaster". This is slightly tempered by an unconfirmed story that Willans was sacked from his teaching post at Carn Brea for swearing at the boys.

THE DIARIES

When Nigel Molesworth began his diaries in August 1939, his school wasn't named, and it was only in July 1940 that it was revealed he was at "St. Cypranes" (Headmaster Mr Trimp).[4] For a brief period in 1940, when St. Cypranes was in "quaranteen", the pupils went to "new skool SunHo", with its "headmaster haf short pants and no cane" (probably modelled on Summerhill and A.S. Neill), and in 1941 Molesworth and his younger brother (Molesworth 2) were sent to a girls' school to be near their father's regiment. ("19 July. Peason write me a p.c. he haf heard I am at a girls skool and ask if I haf been elected most poplar girl. Gosh chiz.").

In October 1941, after St. Cypranes had been bombed ("cheers cheers cheers") it was merged with another school, "St. Guthrums."[5] ("Now we haf TWO headmasters. Am overwhelmed at this thort.") And in 1942 Molesworth spent a

---

3 Quoted in the entry for Geoffrey Willans (written by Mari Prichard) in the *Oxford Dictionary of National Biography.*

4 There has never been a St. Cyprane. However, there was a prep school in Eastbourne, Sussex, called St. Cyprian's, which opened in 1899 and closed, after it was destroyed by a fire, in 1939. Whether or not Geoffrey Willans consciously or subconsciously had this school in mind when he called Molesworth's school St. Cypranes is not known.

5 There has never been a St. Guthrum.

brief period at another girls' school ("St. Ethelburgas").[6] It was not until 1953, with the publication of *Down with Skool!*, that Molesworth found himself permanently at St. Custard's, the school that featured in all the subsequent books.[7]

Of the 20 diary pieces, 12 were set at school, mostly St. Cypranes, with three at St. Guthrums and three at the other schools Molesworth was obliged to attend for brief periods. The remaining eight pieces were set during school holidays, including three at his grandmother's and two at his Aunt Ciss's farm.

The most entertaining of the characters at St. Cypranes is the deaf master (never given a full name) who arrives shortly after war has been declared. He is usually the butt of Molesworth's jokes but is not averse to playing the joker himself. Another entertaining character is "Unckle Bingo," an eccentric practical joker. Other recurring characters include Molesworth's cousin Ermintrude, who is a goody goody and keeps a botany book; Jenkins, who swaps his tonsils for a tooth and 10 of Molesworth's cigarette cards; and, of course, Mr Trimp, Headmaster of St. Cypranes, who comes across as rather more kindly, and far less devious, than St. Custard's Mr Grimes.

The only constant between the diaries and the books, apart from Molesworth and his brother, was the presence of Molesworth's great friend Peason and the unutterably wet and weedy Fotherington-Thomas (who was given the first name David in the diary entry for 7 May 1942 but was named Basil in the books). (The deaf master also appears in the books, but only fleetingly). Of course, there was also Molesworth's

6 St. Ethelburga was the founder and first abbess of Barking Abbey in London.

7 There has never been a St. Custard.

erratic spelling, vague notions of grammar, lack of punctuation, inconsistent capitalisation, and the repetition of certain expressions which quickly became Molesworth trademarks (although not "as any fule kno", which came much later).

Not surprisingly, given the era in which they were written, the main focus of the diaries is the war:

> 1939. 10 November. Air-rade warning. Masters tremble and scram, xcept deaf master who asleep in his room. All boys very heroical and I offer cig card soldier of the british Realm to chap who hear first gun. Peason avacutates white mice which he sa very sussetptible to poson gas. We hear fighting planes – hurricanes – but only deaf master snoring. At last Mr trimp comes and say all into the air-rade shelter all to the shelter dubble. He dash in first (headmasters all the same) and is knee deep in water cheers conduc mark laughing (manners). Very fusty in shelter and white mice perish. We stand on benches but Nazis do not come moan groan they are weedy.

> 1940. 2 March. Catch german measles and peason sa boo weedy german through sickroom door. Haf 1579 spots, not counting back of neck.

School life, of course, had to carry on:

> 1941. 15 January. Chiz chiz chiz haf to go to dancing class. All boys look like girlies and girls haf weedy bows. Misteress sa feeble things she sa now we are all going to be chickens, little cocks and little hens Tippy toes tippy

> toes. Moan and groan. molesworth 2 dance mightily and there fat boy called robin but when he being little cock he fall wam. All larff xcept robin's mother who sa i haf tripped him. Chiz as i do not think anebode see.
>
> 1942. 19 October. Morning bell viz all boys leap from bed at thort of breakfast cheers cheers squadrons of sossages take off from plates and spoons zoom mightily MASTERS sneke in guiltily with yelow faces. Carry out begning of term inspecktion skool dog new bugs skool pig and dirty dick gardners boy all O.K. Test skool dog with trial conker which land in target area but am disgusted to find NEW MASTER who regard me venormously. He sa Hi you what your name: when i say molesworth 1 he sa Har! i haf heard of you. Tremble tremble try old wheeze i.e. look ashamed but no go get 3 conduc marks and when i say gosh 3 sir that a bit stiff he smirk and sa since i not satisfied he will give 4. This is skool record so thank him perlitely and ooze off to chass new bugs.

The last diary entry (in which Molesworth, rather surprisingly, reads F.W. Farrar's lachrymose 1858 school story *Eric, or Little by Little*, and is "deeply impressed") was published on 9 December 1942.

WHAT HAPPENED NEXT

In January 1943 the publisher Collins launched *Collins Magazine for Boys and Girls*, a firmly respectable middle-class monthly (initially only available on subscription) which emphasised the value of reading, and which, for much of its run, attracted some of the best children's writers of the time. In April 1950 its title changed to *Collins Magazine*, and in April 1953 it changed again to *Young Elizabethan*, in a nod to the accession of Queen Elizabeth II. In late 1954, with its circulation dropping, the magazine was bought by John Grigg (the editor of *The National Review* and later Baron Altrincham), who immediately installed Kaye Webb as editor.

Webb had previously been an Assistant Editor at *Lilliput*, and had accepted Ronald Searle's first St. Trinian's cartoon in July 1941 and saw its publication three months later. Famously, Searle, having enlisted in the Royal Engineers in 1939, had been posted abroad shortly before its publication, and only saw it in print when he picked up a copy of the magazine in a street in Singapore in February 1942. Soon after this he was captured by the Japanese and spent over three years as a prisoner-of-war. On his return to England in 1945, he began drawing more St. Trinian's cartoons, which appeared in *Lilliput* and in several books, until, feeling that he had had enough of the school, he decided to stop. However, he reluctantly agreed to collaborate with the humorous writer and newspaper columnist D.B. Wyndham Lewis on a novel, *The Terror of St. Trinian's*, which came out, under the pen-name "Timothy Shy", in October 1952. The publisher, Max Parrish, demanded a sequel for the following year's Christmas market, but Searle refused, and killed off St. Trinian's in an atomic explosion, in the cartoon collection *Souls in Torment*, in 1953.

However, by then Kaye Webb (whom Searle had married in 1948) had introduced him to Geoffrey Willans, and the pair subsequently agreed to collaborate on a new series of Molesworth pieces for a book, which became *Down with Skool!*, published by Max Parrish in October 1953. It sold almost 54,000 copies before the end of the year, and has rarely been out of print since – the second book, *How to be Topp*, followed in the autumn of 1954.

At around the same time, Webb, now installed as editor of the *Young Elizabethan*, commissioned a new series of Molesworth pieces for the magazine, to be illustrated by her husband. The first piece appeared in the January 1955 issue, and further pieces appeared throughout 1955. All of these, with minor textual changes, cuts and additions, were subsequently published in 1956 by Max Parrish in *Whizz for Atomms* (issued in America by the Vanguard Press as *Molesworth's Guide to the Atommic Age*).

Willans and Searle continued contributing Molesworth pieces to the magazine throughout 1956, 1957 and 1958, with almost all of them being gathered together in *Back in the Jug Agane*, published by Max Parrish in late 1958 (dated 1959). Sadly, Willans had died shortly before its appearance.

The first edition of the compilation volume *The Compleet Molesworth* also appeared in the autumn of 1958, published by Max Parrish. A second edition was published by Pavilion Books in 1984, with a foreword by Tim Rice and a note by Ronald Searle. A third edition, under the title *Molesworth*, appeared in 1999, published by Penguin and with an introduction by Philip Hensher; in the following year this was reprinted as a Penguin Classic. The most recent edition of *The Compleet Molesworth* was published by The Folio Society in 2007, with an introduction by Wendy Cope.

READERSHIP

There has been much debate as to whether Molesworth was a character created for an adult or a juvenile readership. His first appearance, in *Punch*, clearly suggests he was originally meant for adults. The first two books were probably aimed at a mixed readership – the publisher, Max Parrish, had issued a wide range of books but little for children, although a clue lies in the sub-title of *Down with Skool!*: "A guide to school life for tiny pupils and their parents." (Having said that, the sub-title of the second book, *How to be Topp*, was "A guide to Sukcess for tiny pupils, including all there is to kno about SPACE"). The third and fourth books were clearly aimed, first and foremost, at a young readership, as their content had originally appeared in a children's magazine. Nevertheless, much of the humour, in all four books, is very knowing and adult, with a sardonic and caustic element far removed from most children's books of the time.

The diaries were far less satirical than the books (although Molesworth's sardonic view of school life and the adult world was fully formed even then), with the satire aimed at the circles Molesworth was moving in: his school(s), his fellow pupils, his relatives and various other adults he encounters, and the army and the Germans. The only world event that intrudes is the war, whereas the books contain countless references to contemporary life – literature, politics, education, class, the space race – which may well have been a mystery to many younger readers. Yet it is known that the books were widely read by children, who took their enthusiasm into adulthood; and it is also worth observing that many of the reprinted editions were published by children's publishers such as Puffin and Armada.

Perhaps the only conclusion to draw is that there is no definitive answer. As Philip Hensher noted in his introduction to *The Compleet Molesworth* in 1999:

> I read these books when I was quite young, probably no more than ten or eleven. Much of the satire passed straight over my head... And yet the intellectual atmosphere of the books was immediately clear: I thought they were children's books when I was a child, and now that I am an adult, I think that they are books for adults about childhood.

TWO SCHOOLS

While Molesworth was at St. Cypranes (mostly) throughout the diaries, and at St. Custard's throughout the run of four books, it was not a seamless transition. The typed manuscript of the first book, *Down with Skool!*,[8] has references to both schools. For example, the opening page, headed "O.K. Come In", refers to Molesworth's school as St. Custard's, whereas in Chapter 5 the description of the school (headed "An Ideal Setting" in the book) refers to St. Cypranes, as does the caption to the drawing of the Honours Board a few pages later. The sequence of "photographs" from the Molesworth Album at the beginning of the typescript features the deaf master, although

8 The typescript, complete with Ronald Searle's rough sketches, was retained by Max Parrish and then given to an employee of the firm. Along with a dummy copy of *The Terror of St. Trinian's*, it was auctioned at Toovey's, in West Sussex, on 13 August 2019, the two items selling for £7,117 (including the buyer's premium) to Modern First Editions, a bookdealer in Ilkley, West Yorkshire. The typescript was subsequently advertised at £12,500 and was acquired by the Houghton Library at Harvard University, Massachusetts, USA (MS Typ 1289).

this was omitted from the published version. And in the pictorial sequence "A Few Headmasters", one of the sketches is captioned "Come on, St. Cypranes", with "Cypranes" crossed out and "Custards" written in pencil above.

It is impossible to know why the original draft of *Down with Skool!* had references to both schools – whether or not Willans was in two minds when he wrote it, or whether he had settled on St. Custard's at the outset, as suggested by the opening page of the original typescript, and simply forgot as the text developed. That is assuming, of course, that the opening page was written before everything else.

CRITICISM

There has been very little in the way of critical comment on the diaries, presumably because they are so little-known. Where they are known, opinion has usually been negative. In 1992, Kevin Jackson wrote in the *Independent*, "When *Punch*, RIP, reprinted some of Willans's earliest Molesworth pieces a few years ago, most readers were bitterly disappointed – they were rather dull, hard to read, and lacked the superb timing of the four main books." In her introduction to The Folio Society edition, Wendy Cope commented that they were "nowhere near as good as the books," but she added that they were "instructive reading for a writer. They show just how much improvement can be brought about as a result of time, thought and revision."

There is an element of truth in this, in that the books were a result of Willans not only honing his craft but expanding his horizons, and moving away from a straightforward narrative of events which formed the diaries' basis. (It is also true that

Ronald Searle's illustrations added another dimension.) But the diaries are still important in that they are an introduction to Molesworth. Willans plunges straight into his world without any sort of preamble – Nigel Molesworth appears fully formed, with all the hallmarks that make him a unique character firmly in place.

The main difference is that the books gave full reign to Molesworth's subversive (and surprisingly sophisticated) view of the world. As Alexandra Mullen, in *The Encyclopedia of British Humorists* (1996), observed:

> The Molesworth of the books is a more fully developed and canny character than the Molesworth who first appeared in *Punch*, largely because Willans recast Molesworth's voice from the unwittingly comic one of the diaries to a more knowingly sardonic one.

A similar view came from Robin Blake in the magazine *Slightly Foxed* (issue 21, March 2009) when he wrote that the diaries gave Willans "a main character, a setting and a rich fund of ideas for his subsequent post-war collaboration with the cartoonist Ronald Searle".

Unlike other fictional comic prep school boys of his era – Donald Gilchrists's Seeley-Bohn, Klaxon's Aloysius, Anthony Buckeridge's Jennings, and the boys in H.F. Ellis's A.J. Wentworth stories – where much of the humour comes from the clash between a child's view of the world and an adult's view, Molesworth is on a different plane. He has a knowing and cynical view of the world which is more adult than childish, and this gives the humour a satirical bite that elevates it to a level far higher than that of simple farce or comedy. While this is less evident in the diaries, the seeds are clearly there.

After Geoffrey Willans's death, Ronald Searle wrote in *The Times* (9 August 1958) that "Willans was the sort of writer who made collaboration sheer enjoyment. The characters which sprang from his invention were funny, not merely because of the clarity with which they were observed, but also because of the wickedly penetrating insight he had into human nature." He went on to describe Molesworth as his most successful literary creation, "whose cunning was more refined than that of Bunter, and who concealed behind his misspelt observations of life all the wiles of a diplomat in foreign affairs".

He added that "Willans was delighted to learn that schoolmasters, far from feeling publicly disrobed, were, in fact, giving away his books as end-of-term prizes."

Coo, gosh (as Molesworth himself might have said).

ROBERT J. KIRKPATRICK

EDITOR'S NOTE

THE DIARIES HAVE been carefully transcribed from the original issues of *Punch* in which they first appeared. Of course, my computer's spell check and grammar check were completely useless with the original transcribed text, being riddled with red and green underlinings, until the point at which the checking process ground to an exhausted halt. It is, however, hoped that the text published here is exactly that which appeared in *Punch* (the only exceptions being two wholly unnecessary punctuation marks that appeared in the original text and were, possibly, errors by the typesetter rather than deliberately included by Geoffrey Willans). In any case, if any variations from the original have crept in, it is an odds-on certainty that no-one will notice, and Geoffrey Willans would surely be forgiving…

THE DIARIES OF NIGEL MOLESWORTH

As published in *Punch*, 1939–1942

1939

Punch, 9 August 1939

MY SUMER DIARY

Contains:
TIME-TABLES OF DIFFERENT SITUATONS
and
of SPORT and mainly
A running commentary on spiecial days.

May 6.

Arrived back at school. Started to cry and went into jim to wear it off. Ragged in jim but was stoped by Mr Trimp (headmaster) and recived conduc mark chiz. Rember have some cigs in plabox and endevore to remove them but Mr Oates (geog) sees me and says what have you got there, nothing sir honestly, I say you can see if you want to sir. He say I trust you molesworth but he follow me when I go out chiz. Will have to wait. Went on raging and mucked about and after tea went and had reeding Mr Trimp read Dr syn. Quite a good book every body gets murded. Mr Trimp says it will be fine tomow.

May 7.

It rained.

What have you got there

May 27.
Morning frightful lessons. Weedy french Way Mr Trimp tells us to rember this

je suis	I am a pot of jam
Tu a	he is a botle of fizz
Il est	thou art an apple tart etc.:

Played cricket blowed three wide 8 no-balls. Caught Jenkins with a catch great cheers rose. I am in fuste but have my cigs and slosh in order to get out. Hit boundary and Mr Oates says well hit but keep a strate bat. I was l.b.w. (it shot) and take cigs into rodendhon bushes but Mr Oates shout what are you doing in there molesworth. Catching may bugs i reply. He belive me (sap) but not worth it to light cigs then. Borrow Peasons bat it has three springs and play tip and run. I like foopball bes.

June 6.
Gibbon monkeys cry is this Wah Wah.

June 17.
Arith and geom both fowl, had jim lesson in breack with Sergent Bubble. His son came and taught us quite diffrent from what the other peoply had taught us, Cigs fell out of my poket and Mr oates see them who hapned to be by; he looked at me. I think he suspecks. Drawing in afternoon I drew a ship and when it was painted it looked awful chiz.

June 23.

Bathing in morning Did a bellyfloper and came in gasping.

Did a bellyfloper

Bubble's son went for swum afterwards (very hairy?) Tryd to smoke cigs with Jenkins but forgot matches. As mr Oates to lend me his box to try to light a scout fire but he came and showed me. Set fire to Jenkins braces which were under twigs. He say I put them there on purpose and make me write out Lars possena of clussium etc: Mr Trimp blew me up about braces he says it will be fine tomow.

June 24.

Sleet and showers.

June 28.

Had dream. Three dieing masters lie on their beds go home no wone to teach us cheers. Cheers. Return home sweet home it made me weep with joy. Buy som Bullseyes, come out sucking them, then get penny worth of Speamint. Fight village boys and overcome them then woke up chiz. Pearson snores.

July 3.

Unfortunately I report gum boil on a tooth which was under Matron's eye or at least has been for some time and I have got to go the dentist, Mr Pringle. Mr Pringle say tooth to come out. It felt very queer when they put the bag over my mouth I went strait to sleep. Keep tooth but swap it with Jenkins. I give him tooth and ten cig cards (battleships) for his tonsils.

July 10.

When I went to look at the paper, actually the "Daily Telegraph" I was amazed to see Sandstar was beaten by Daily Worker a head. So I think Daily Worker my choice for Lewes. Tush who I do not think still happens to be hot favourate, but I don't like it still. Geom with Stinker (Mr Cutler) Don't know anything drew an example like this

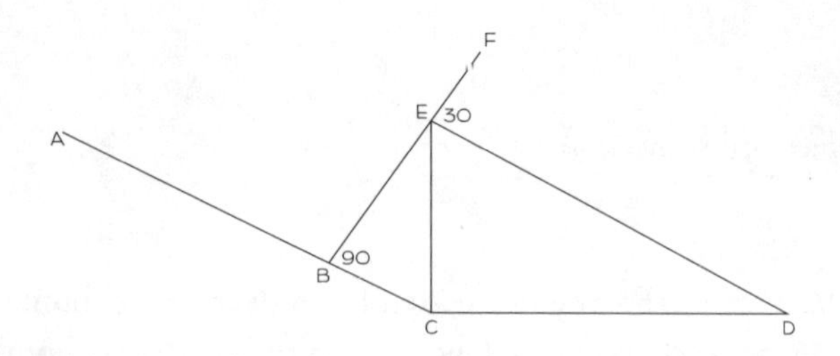

Find remaning angles, got blown sky high because didn't know.

July 17.

My granny's got wrinkles in her face.

My granny.

July 19.

In afternoon went out with a person, Aunt Ciss actually. I eat bread and jam, eclair macaroon and ice. Then strubres. Felt sick when I came back and mr Oates look at me and say haf you been smoking. No I say so boo. Conduc mark very impertnent behaviour. Miss prep anyway cheers cheers.

August 1.

Everyone is terribly excited by the end of term including myself and the masters and misteresses and Sergent Bubbles son. Dogs, birds, babys, Tortorsis and nearly every living thing in the school. I pack dead bird (thrush) in my plabox it didn't half smell also tank bristol bomber and Jenkins tonsils. Jenkins quizzed my tooth and I said ego and will give it decent berrial with the thrush. Find cigs again and determine to smoke them. Go to shooting range and haf just put cig in my mouth when mr oates pounces out it is only choclat sir i say so boo he say what a good imitation and I ask him to eat them which he did. He then take me to Mr Trimp and I got 6 chiz but it was worth it. Show marks to Peason. Mr Trimp says it will be sunny tomow.

August 2.

It snowed.

Punch, 27 December 1939

MY DIARY OF THE WAR

Contains: Time-Tables of War days and a.R.p. Huns, boshes, Nazis dirty roters and tuoughs.

Sept. 3.

War declared. 3 tuoughs arrive from Bermingham who are put in Spare room thay are awful. They pute out there tongues at me so when mum not looking i scrap them. Chiz. They overcome me but oldest blub and sa he tell his ma. others say ya sissie then oldest hit them and all blub. Ern say his father is a rober (swank) Arch runs about with no trousis he is not going to be a gentlman and at cricket they all slosh and touogh each other up.

Sept. 16

Uncle come in uniform weedy private. Now i say you will haf to kill as many germans as the last war and as that was 5000 you will be hard pute to it. Uncle tell how he kaptured ten germans on the Som but Ern creep up and let off toy pistle with cap and uncle jump like anything three feet actually. He chase Ern who hide in walnut tree but give Arch 6 Cheers Ern say his father a murderer he murded 3 old ladies in their bath and strwth the blud was awful.

Sept. 19.

Arch has catpillar he was tamed.

Sept. 24.

Back to school weedy school. Peason and me rage in the jim and he say stinker (Mr Cutler) and Sergent Buble also gone to join up which is enough to pute the germans off. mr Trimp (headmaster) still here but new master is awful as he deaf and face like a monky. Schwarz, german boy say war is just british propergander and hitler win india paris and magninot line. Deaf master agree with him but i do not think he hear. Fotherington-tomas has brought back fairy cycle weedy. Mr trimp say poland not really beaten.

Sept. 25.

7760400 secs to end of term.

Sept. 30.

Trouble with deaf master. He tell us joke caesar had some jam for tea (funny?) and laugh like anything but i draw tremdous tank on a new piece of blotch and he got batey. Write out AMo mono and rego from shorter eating primer. Sergent Bublys son (jimmnasticks) and take us for jewsitsui. He throw Peason over his head.

Nov. 10.

Aire-rade warning. Masters tremble and scram, xcept deaf master who alseep in his room. All boys very heroical and I offer cig card solder of the british Realm to chap who hear first gun. Pearson avacutates white mice which he sa very sussetptible to poson gas. We hear fighting planes — hurricanes — but only deaf master snoring. At last Mr trimp comes and say all into the air-rade shelter all to the shelter dubble. He dash in first (headmasters all the same) and is knee deep in water cheers conduc mark laughing (manners). Very fusty in shelter and white mice perish. We stand on benches but nazis do not come moan groan they are weedy.

Nov. 18.

Schwarz has face like a stuffed tomato.

Nov. 20.

The new bugs are like girlies awful ticks. They hold hands with deaf master and also Mr trimp and mr Oates (geog). they belive in faires and santa claus. They tell deaf master stories about Snow Wite and the 7 dwarffs and he say they are delightful (sap) Deaf master rember about deten amo moneo rego and give me twice chiz. I get new bugs in croner and make them scarp Schwarz. He say wait till hitler gets to London:

Nov. 23.

For school concert we do Hamlet and i am Ophelia chiz chiz chiz.

Nov. 29.

Unfortunately we play foopball match against St Olafs and loose eight goals to 0. I was amazed at st. Olaf headmster who shout lustily 'keep it going st Olafs. He's holding up the whole side is Titmarsh mi. Schwarz lets goals through and we tough him each time, especially Isaacs. Tea cheers tea dough nuts and sardines also macaroons. Matron says Peason no longer to keep dead mice in his colar box so we bury them at sea in air-rade shelter.

Dec. 9.
950400 secs to end of term.

Dec. 12.

Peason is hamlet

School concert chiz. Peason is hamlet and i haf to blub like anything when he tell me to go into a nunery. Axcident sergent buble's son pull curtain too soon when Mr trimp smaking ghost's head. Absolute snubs. Wish i was a gost all the same I would haunt everybody. Deaf master fuses lights (general Fotherington-tomas too close to Mrs Trimp after?) Get prize water babies general progress chiz. Swap water babies for anti-aircraft gun and micky mouse weekly.

Dec. 13.

Deaf master ask for deten amo moneo rego and say his patience nearly exorsted.

Dec. 16.

Today all school learn to knit for the soldiers. We do squares and Mrs Trimp stitch into blanket but I am unable actually as I cannot two purl one plane for toffee. Will make my square into balaklava helmet for Aunt Ciss who in the land Army for Christmas Give Isaacs two cig cards (swaps) to do my deten for deaf master. Peason makes water babies into darts and I get blown up chiz.

Dec. 20.

Troublesom rags, pillow fights and toughery. We sing song no more latin no more french no more sitting on hard old bench and school dog bite Swarchz. Pack plabox and water babies, pen knife and kniting for Aunt Ciss. As i draw mr Trimp's face on board deaf master say what about deten amo moneo rego. I show him what Isaacs had written but he has done wrong stuff moan and jasper. Deaf master say he is very tired of waiting and i say 'honestly honour bright I will send it in the hols' He say that is very straightforward of me (sap). Mr trimp say it will snow tomow.

Dec. 21.

glorious sunny day yar boo and sucks to the masters. Hurra for Xmas.

Punch, 21 February 1940

MOLESWORTH THE GOOD

Contains: Time-Tables of hols, girls, rats, farms and good conduc.

Dec. 29.

Down to stay at Aunt Ciss farm for rest of hols chiz. Aunt ciss meet us in britches also weedy girl called ermintrude and avakuee called Ivy. Who is a titch. They sa where is your brother. I sa i do not kno honest injun but he was here a minit ago and they find him in lugage rack blubbing. molesworth II sa I haf pute him there. He is a sneke and just because he coming to school nex term he swanks and mucks about. He is absolutely weedy.

Dec. 30.

All girls are weedy, espeshally ermintrude.

Dec. 31.

There is a tuough bull here called Jack it is ferce and i tie bunch of carrots to its tale. Molesworth II sa go it and then snekes to aunt Ciss chiz and she sa sit quietly with ermintrude chiz chiz chiz. Ermintrude is goody goody she loves pritty flowers and doesnt muck about with her food. She sa it is rude to make lake in mashed potatoes with gravy. She likes prunes (swank). Tonite Aunt ciss read us a book eric or little by little which is not bad actually, Ermintrude sa why can't you be good like that.

1940

Jan. 1.

New Year resoution detmin to be GOOD.

Jan. 2.

Try out my catterpult and see Aunt Ciss in her britches. Refrane. Then molesworth II come up and sa "you haf a face like a squashed tomatoe." When i do not tuough him up he sa it like a trillion squashed tomatoes. At tea I wash hands and some of face. Ermintrude sa i look more human. Chiz? She is not bad actually. She haf missed sunda school for 3 years. Coo.

Jan. 3.

Aunt ciss give us party and we pla postmans knock chiz chiz chiz weedy. I call out little girl with pink ribon but when she sees me she blub and run away. molesworth II go out but when he do not call anebody aunt ciss find him in the larder eating jelly. He tie ermintrude's pigtale to xmas tree and get sent to bed. Absolute snubs. I hide under sofa to avoid dancing actually and find ivy there. I sit on her tofees but she sa garn she like them better with hairs on.

Jan. 4.

Find topping dead rat in one of the lofts and molesworth II sa I can give him two sloshes for it. no i sa you can haf it for nothing.

Find topping dead rat

He sa thanks awfully then call me measly flea and rune away. Gratitude? at nite I find rat in bed and rise full of wrath to slorter him but rember i am good. All the same will tuough him up when I stop. Put rat tidily in wash-basin but friten maid in morning when she come and she haf hystericks. Aunt Ciss give me 6 with hairbrush chiz. Ermintrude ignore me.

Jan. 7.

Ermintrude is peculiar she do lessons in the hols for fun and dances weedily. She give me her autograff book as favour were everone had written weedy things like cheerio gwen. I draw fat person aunt Ciss but change it into cow. Ermintrude get batey and sa she will not let me see her botany Book now. She praktise piano fairy dance awful. I sa not bad and she call me Sir galahad. Unfortunately Molesworth II hapned to be by on way to larder and he larff like anything. He is weedy and swanks just becos he haf septick spots.

Jan. 11.

Aint ciss take us to panto in her old grid. jack and the beanstalk rather weedy as they all fall in love. molesworth II flick toofee papers on peoply downstairs and Ivy eat orange. molesworth II buy pips for a d. and bombs downstairs like anything. Aunt ciss give him 6d for hitting mrs fulkington-Brown. Ermintrude aloof but she sa the faires are beautiful: widow Twanky say dam and ivy larff so much she choke and swallow pip.

Jan. 12.

Snow. Detmin to STOP being good.

Jan. 13.

Toda i will tuough up the bull, hide aunt ciss britches snoball ermintrude and teach molesworth II sharp lesson. Go out mightily to carry out plans ree bull. and coolect coollossal snoball but bull turn and lick my hand and i haf not the heart. It is not a bad bull so detmin to throw snoball at molesworth II insted. Find him coolecting bad words from bill the labourer in harnes room. Wam bonk throw ball but hit bill. Molesworth II learn new words. Ivy come in highly delighted she haf lost her pants but ermintrude practise greek dance indoors. I think she is mouldy after all.

Jan. 15.

Moan groan can't seem to stop being good. Must do better. Ermintrude come into sno but pla girly games. She sa eenee meenee miny mo and wallflowers wallflowers grow so tall but ermintrude is the strongest and out you must go. molesworth II pla but chizzes and sa he haf not been tagged. Ermintrude sa sliding is comon but skating graceful. She swank she can skate so we find pond with thin ice and she fall in splosh. Aunt Ciss sa what a shame then give us sixpence. She is sporting.

Jan. 17.

Molesworth II teech bills words to the parot but parot tell him off. Parot is Chapel.

Jan. 20.

Rover the sheepdog dig up rat so i prepare trap for molesworth II, pute it in his bed also holly and buket of water on door. Then I sa fetch the air gune molesworth II o you might and he go off but meet ermintrude who sa she always happy to rune an erand. Molesworth II sa okay and while he gone he steal her butter rashon. Water fall on ermintrude and she sa I am a beastly beast and she will never let me see her botany Book. Don't want to so boo. molesworth II discover rat and offer it to parrot. Parrot use one of bill's words and ivy come back wet as she haf sat down in pudle. All sent to bed.

Jan. 24.

Back to school weedy school. Moan and jasper. Packing and all sad even bull and parrot. Bull roars and i give it old carrot but Ivy blub becos it was hers. Parrot sing Polly pute the ketle on which it only do under stress of great emotion. Sa goodby and off to station in old grid. Molesworth II sa he will take photo of ermintrude but when he click camera out fly rat on spring.

Molesworth II sa he will take photo of ermintrude but when he click camera out fly rat on spring.

Train comes in express called corfe Castle 4–6–2 streamlined. chuff chuff wizz wave to aunt ciss and put molesworth II in lugage rack. Settle down to micky mouse weekly. Boo to school.

Jan. 25.
7267354 secs to end of term.

Punch, 10 April 1940

MOLESWORTH DETECTIVE

Contains: Diary of sloothes, chizzes, measels, drones, groans and moans.

March 1.
Mr trimp (headmaster) say all to xsemble in big skool and we all think Peason to get cane on account of white mouse

in deaf master's bed. Sit back gloating but no cane chiz. mr Trimp sa buter rashon haf dispeared from boot room. He sa he do not suspeck anebode but look at me chiz so do Mr oates — time he joined up? but I am incent. Noone sa so will track buter:

Suspecks
1. schwarz, german boy (sabotarge)
2. molesworth 2
3. Skool dog.
4. deaf master.

March 2.

Catch german measels and peason sa boo weedy german through sickroom door. Haf 1579 spots, not counting back of neck. Nothing to do draw mr Trimp and change into rose to match wallpaper. Weedy new bug in next bed he arsk me to tell him faire story chiz tell him a tuough one and he blub for mummy. Squadron of cats zoom about watch skool dog. It dig for moles; and sometimes lie on its back exorsted. When mr Trimp call it slink away. Do not think it gilty of buter rashon not tuough enough.

March 10.

Back to skool chiz moan but matron say i look peeky (ass?) molesworth 2 is weedy and Miss pringle (kindgarden) do not like him. She show him leafs and flowers and read stories for the want-to be read tos but he sa they are weedy. She read poems about gnomes and pixies but he only interested in Spinach, his monky and other dollys. He make nest for monkys in skool museum in coco beans prersented by Majer

Forterskew. He is wonky. schwarz german boy is wonky to he orgnise new bugs into german bund.

March 11.

Walk with deaf master weedy crocodile and he point out birds with walking stick. Boo to coots and blackbirds. Titch follow us from vilage skool. Deaf master tell him to go away but he just grin. he sa to deaf master garn not fair big boots. Cheers. Fotherington-tomas who pick crocusses want to walk hand in hand with titch and this scare him away. Fotherington-tomas is a girly and proud he can skip. Chuck lump of mud at him quietly and he blub. Deaf master comfort him but he rune away. mighty cheers from all. Buzz wizard brick on tin roof.

March 12.

Mr trimp sa stout finns will never sign peace. Rumour he to be called up for ministry of Information. Gloat.

March 16.

Track schwarz for buter rashon but he only throw stone at deaf master and hit him on the nut. Tuough cheddar on deaf master actually. schwarz is weedy and he cant pla foopball for toofee he always chasses goalkeeper or stands on his head. See molesworth 2 going to pig stys where he pot at pigs. Track him but he see me and shout flea flea anti-me then rune away.

March 21.

Leckture by Majer Forterskew War as i see it feeble. He haf

red nose and when fotherington-tomas see him he blubs loudly and haf to go to matron. Absolute snubs. Deaf master put in slides all upside down and never hear when majer Forterskew click. Weedy slides, no blud, tanks or aeroplanes and all germans are alive. Mr trimp make speech and sa he sorry majer forterskew going away, but deaf master think it three cheers and cheer lustily. Wizard tea mackeroons. Take record bite.

March 22.

Tuough trouble Majer Forterskew haf seen molesworth 2 monkys in his coco beans and blow up. Molesworth 2 tells whoper and sa it was me he is an absolute roter just becos i bag his dinkytoy. Punishment clean out skool museum. Find old cake, Jenkins tonsils and mr Oates (geog) jim shoe. Deaf master come along and sa coco beans jolly interesting. I arsk about old cake and he sa rare green fungus sap. He is bats.

March 23.

Miss pringle and curate are sweteharts. Hem. Hem.

March 24.

Parents day and Peason's mother comes very fat. She smell of scent poo gosh and call peason darling he is a girly. Mr trimp prowl nervously like skool dog he smile at Peason all teeth and call me Nigel (christan name) chiz chiz chiz chiz. Mrs Peason fondle Peason's ears and schwarz sa we deckadent nation doomed to xtinction. Isaacs take out schwarz for set of cig. cards (battleships) now rare and dead frog.

March 25.

Life is odd sometimes.

March 27.

Read topping tale in prep man with red skull. Deaf master cob me and give me deten and conduc mark (deceit) write out poem e.g. harfleag harfleag harfleag onward rode the 3000. Haf old copy in english book so tear out and take up careful chizzing. Room ponk of tobaco and in middle deaf masters favrite box. Inspect box and find BUTER painted on it. Tell Peason who bet me million pounds i am wrong bet him million trillion back. It is deaf masters half day when he haf tea at cozy teashop (stuffs cream cakes?) so open box and find old socks. Absolute chiz. Peason nasty about million trillion pounds and sa it no fair I feigned fingers crossed. He demand payment so give him soldier (german fighting troops) belonging to schwarz. schwarz sa just like england

April 1.

April fools day will chiz all masters and misteresses also skool dog. Will pin kick me on deaf masters back. Awate oppertunity but deaf master sa haf i not seen aeroplane crash on big field. Dash out but nothing there. Chiz chiz chiz grind teeth and buzz aple at skool pig instead. Peason votes we stick draring pin on deaf masters chair revenge but he come too soon and there shouts of K.V. Sit down in place on draring pin. Drone. Deaf master highly delighted he haf placed it there and give us lesson on how to win the war.

April 2.

End of term cheers cheers pack tuckboxs. Everbode happy and quizz ego everything. Isaacs swap skool piano with fortherinton-tomas for camera. (browne No 2). All to big skool where mr Trimp sa we all pleased to know that majer forterskew haf presented at begning of term dead snake to skool museum. He open box but buter rashon inside. Absolute snubs. Where is snake? Isaacs sa he haf found one and sold to gardners boy. He gets 6. Mr trimp sa bound to rain tomow.

April 3.

Sun shines glorously. We are all very big fools and we don't like skool at all.

Punch, 15 May 1940

MOLESWORTH AND THE WICKED GRANDMOTHER

Contains: Time-Table of grandmothers,
choc-bars, cats and tuough times
ALSO
Runing comentary on ernest the dog.

April 6.

Mum tell us we to go to granny molesworth for rest of hols. Absolute chiz as she haf a face like a monky and is also record bossy. Molesworth 2 blub and sa he going to die so give him buble gum, also biskit crums from pocket and tooffee that was sticking on penknife. Pack trunk i.e. dead frog, dinkytoys of all sorts and bat (three springs). Skool report arrive hem hem and mum sa phew. She do not kno what Pa will sa. Will stuff silk hankercheif down trousis as Peason bet it break canes.

April 7.

Silk hankerchiefs do NOT break canes. Q.E.D.

April 8.

Set off in cranky old grid. moleworth 2 bag front seat he is a swanker and when we turn always pute out hand wrong way. Crash bang and colonel zoom up with red nose absolutely batey. He sa he crushed both wings and chowfeur call him blooming (?) buterfly. He drive off shaking fist and molesworth 2 cop him with an orange. Gran to meet us she is weedier than ever and make us wipe boots and noses.

April 9.

Gran very stricked she make us not cut mashed potatoes into squares and forts chiz. molesworth 2 sulk as he sailing a bean into a mighty fjord. Gran sa when she a girl she very beatiful and moleworth 2 sa i bet. Butler laff so much he drob rubarb on carpet. Chiz as gran won't let me eat it. She is weedy and haf weedy cat and ernest a dog who amaze me. It haf little yelow coat and thinks it is tuough becos it die for the king.

April 11.

Tea party. Tons of fusty old lades and we haf to pute on eton colars chiz chiz chiz. Silence while molesworth 2 pla piano "Faire bells." Dog ernest howls and cat spring through window. All lades sa deliteful and knit furously so molesworth 2 pla again. "Charge of mountane ponies." All take cover while he pla mightily. Then he do tricks from our boys conjerring outfit. He take card out of mrs maplethorpe vicars wifes ear. Chiz as anebode could see he had it in his hand (also hair and part of mrs Maplethorpe hat).

April 16.

Pa come down cheers cheers. We pla cricket on crokey lawn and he is absolutely rotten. Bowl him fuste ball with cunning guglie also molesworth 2 but he sa he not looking chiz. Mum then bowl i prepare to slosh mightily but she bowl dolly all along ground. Terf explode everwhere bat hit ernest (dog) and he die for king immediately. Pa then take wizard swipe. Wizz wam ball hit greenhouse. Grandmothers, gardners cooks and dogs rush into air-rade shelter, expecially butler as whisky kept there. Gran appear on horizon at last and Pa go quickly off to pub (Beer?) leaving mum to face musick. Not the way to win war.

April 17.

Gran sa we to haf grate treat but she only read chatterbox chiz. She think same absolutely funny and chuckle like anything but record weedy as all girls good and boys like clergymen no blud short squat pistols or men from mars. Molesworth 2 sa jolly good but he only sitting under piano tearing hairs out of ernest dog. Gran think molesworth 2 wonderful and he sit on her knee becos he kno she give him 6d. He is feeble. At dinner Gran start chuckling and sa she remembed something in chatterbox. Coo.

April 20.

Cat still missing after molesworth 2 pla faire bells at tea party.

April 21.

Another grate treat chiz taken to see weedy cathedral. Not bad actually as some topping tombs and gran sa skeltons underneath. Shiver. Also man with 20 children. GOSH. Gran tired so give me 6d. to see cloysters but sneke out and buy chocbars from stope-me. Bars melt in poket but the taste is not disagreeable but gran cop me and sent to bed with bread and water. Molesworth 2 highly delited he haf my share of custard also wizard cutlet yum-yum but absolute snubs after as gran read long story in chatterbox. She is weedy and sa feeble things i.e. little boys should be seen and not heard and food hot becos it come from hot place.

April 23.

Molesworth 2 is weedy he zoom about pretending to be a wellington bomber and go ah-ah-ah (machine gun fire)

Molesworth 2 pretending to be a wellington bomber

He sa he haf shot down butler cook and ernest the dog also chowfeur who haf black smoke issuing when he dispeared into a cloud. molesworth 2 then return safely to his base. Gran challenge me to crokey but no balls as molesworth 2 use them for heavy bombs. Find balls in best tulip bed also ernest dog stuned. Pla crokey but gran beat me hollow chiz. She highly delited and whack my ball miles.

April 25.

Cat still absent and gran worred. molesworth 2 sa he haf eaten it but no wone belive him as he always tell wopers. Gran ring up police, also sharpen knives and call puss puss. If i were a cat i wouldn't come back. Fly aeroplane but it go strate into ground. Give lacky 500 turns and plane make wizard flite through gran's window hem hem. She leap out of bed as she think it bat which get in her hair. 3 weedy ones with sliper didn't hurt so boo.

April 29.

molesworth 2 is a fool and knos 0.

May 3.

Mr trimp (skool headmaster) write to sa skool closed becos of quaranteen and great cheers rise. We leap for joy but gran sa we go to another school. CHEEZ. Prepare to go gran give me 2/6 and molesworth 2 only get chatterbox snubs. Climb into cranky old grid and cat flash by. It see molesworth 2 and dash up monky tree. Brrh brrh car starts 20 h.p. mighty engine roaring. All wave and ernest (dog) rush after barking and die for king blocking road. Molesworth 2 thro chatterbox and he rune off to berry it. Good riddance to grandmothers.

May 4.

Will tuough all boys at new skool.

Punch, 3 July 1940

MOLESWORTH THE PROBLEM CHILD

Contains: Diary of new skools, weeds, swots, may bugs and belyflopers

May 3.

St Cypranes is in quaranteen so we go to new skool SunHo. The headmaster amaze me he haf short pants and no cane. molesworth 2 larff like anything but no conduc mark and headmaster pat him on head chiz. Headmaster sa we to call him bill he is absolutely bats as it would be cheeky. Outside on lawn many boys in trousis only and more masters in short pants. Also headmaster's mother who haf face like a nanny gote.May 4.

May 4.

All boys wake up early and dance in the dew, also headmaster and headmasters mother. molesworth 2 leap about mightily and offer to pla faire bells on piano. Brekfast absolutely weedy nuts and raw carots chiz no bacon frizzly sosages hony toste or marmalade. molesworth 2 blub he sa he hungry so bag pot of radio malt and give to him also balzum of hony and bottle of pills. We haf feast molesworth 2 eat six pills phew. He sa they taste of acid drops. We greatly refreshed and tuough all boys up at least i do as molesworth 2 only jump about and sa go it. All here are consheentous objecters also headmasters mother and do not like blud.

Molesworth 2 leap about mightily and offer to pla faire bells on piano.

May 10.
Swoters are roters.

May 15.
This skool is bats and noone do any work except kniting for troops and weedy english e.g., poems which all praise weedily they swoon with joy. I knit sock but drop all stiches and cyril sneer in konsequece chiz. he swank he knit oil socks easy as pie and make 10 rafia bags. All boys toady to him becos he knit so well. molesworth 2 sa he make 10000000 rafia bags all at home but all sa shut up swanking.

May 20.
Skool pla to do paradise Lost and i am an angel Coo.

May 25.

Receive letter from jenkins. He sa st. Cypranes still in quarenteen but he at home. He haf cofee mackaroons ices yum yum and frizzly sosages it make my mouth water. He sa he know a boy who give him good offer for his tonsils in spite of second hand. He arsk me to pack them registered post but i reply findings keepings.

May 27.

No criket here chiz chiz chiz and moleswroth 2 tell all boys how he a mighty blower and done hat trick seven times. He show boy Cyril actually and charge up field from skool maypole like grampus. Absolute snubs as ball go back over his head and stun headmasters mother who gathering rose petals for madcap carnival of all boys chiz. Absolutely weedy as only dance round skool maypole and skip weedily like girlies. Tie up 2 masters with ribons and molesworth 2 trip headmasters mother as she leap through the air. Grate confusion and we not allowed herb tea. Don't want any so boo.

May 31.

Terence who is a sneke arsk me if I am a coomunist. Chiz? Molesworth 2 who hapned to be by sa Yes and all praise him. molesworth 2 sa he bigest coomunist in the world in the sky in the universe. Cyril sa i bet and molesworth 2 sa Am. They sa am: not: am: not: am: not: am and molesworth 2 sa i am actually and cyril sa not ten times quickly. He is feeble so tuough him up altho he sa pax. Headmaster call me up and sa i haf paranoiack tendencys. He arsk if i ever felt i wanted to be a house painter he is bats. No dogs pigs or tortosis here as they unhygic only statues of lades called Pysic very beatiful no doubt.

June 1.

un shine glorously and all go to lake including headmasters mother with green costume she think she like Pysic. Do six wizard belyflopers, ducks all boys and gargle water like wale. molesworth 2 swank weedily he can swim but do not feel like it today, As i dry he rune up with headmasters short pants. He sa he give them to me chiz. Moan drone hide pants in rabit hole. Whistle blows all boys to rally where are pants and all look at me chiz. Headmaster sa dishonourable to steal headmasters pants the work of ptenshial enemy of society. He sa he give them to me freely and stork off with no trousis. Am pute in coventry and cyril expel me from litry gild and sa i not to read bernard shaw cheers cheers as only joined for the food.

June 5.

Have 16 dead may bugs in box. poo gosh.

June 8.

Try to sell headmasters pants in vane. He haf a new pair now they are mauve and all masters congratulate him. Skool play paradise lost in rose garden. Moleswroth 2 is spirit of milton (poet) but when he speke prolog he get bashful and rune away. He offer to pla faire bells insted. absolute chiz being angel as not allowed to flap wings and only one word to sa Lo. Tie headmasters pants to Archfiends tail and buzz old conker at molock.

June 9.

In coventry agane.

June 10.

Mum send wizard aeroplane (Wellington bomber). Out of coventry.

June 15.

Hole skool to rose garden to greet the sumer. All sing skool song composed by headmasters mother, e.g.

> Awake SunHo and with thy fellow
> Salute skool colors blew, black and yelow.

Terence sa three cheers for mrs Pettigrew after and moleswroth 2 sa hip hip boo. Then headmaster sa to award prize to most popular boy. Get three votes moleswroth 2 new bug Plunket and ME (hem hem). Terence is elected chiz and headmasters mother put crown of laurel on brow. Also he get weedy book by karl Marks and kiss from headmasters wife. (Not bad actually). Hem-hem agane.

June 16.

Two inches of sock completed at kniting.

June 17.

Letter from mum saying st Cypranes is out of quarenteen cheers cheers and we go back tomow. We leap for joy and molesworth 2 so grateful he offer to me german heinkel for change and i can shoot him down. We zoom about going ah-ah-ah (machine gune fire) till master sa stop o please stop really, his nerves won't stand it he is a girly and haf curls.

Two inches of sock

June 18.

All packed and Cyril give us large daisy chain mementoe of boys. Give him six dead may bugs though it hurt me to do so. Headmaster sa he hope we been happy and boy Plunket new bug rush up blubbing he sa he want to go to. Car come. All cheer skool song SunHo says farewell, Headmasters mother wipes eyes Goodby goodby.

June 19.

St Cypranes agane and molesworth 2 give me headmasters mauve trousis he sa he found them. French weedy french. Ou est papa rat. Boo to papa rat and all masters.

Punch, 20 November 1940

MOLESWORTH AND THE BATTLE OF BRITAIN

Diary of booms, whizzes, wams, explodings and headmasters.

Oct. 30.

I am called to mr Trimp (headmasters) study and all chortle they think I get the kane. Deaf master step out from behind stuffed bear and sa haha. Chiz knock on door and find Gran there chiz chiz chiz. Would rather have the kane. Also pop in uniform but only weedy kaptain so dare not show him as new bugs father a General. Gran sa molesworth 2 and me to go to Canda weedy as no bombs there. Pop and mr Trimp sa this is not allowed but Gran refuse to belive she sa she will see to it herself. Mr trimp offer pop a sherry (n.b. very like his daily tonic for the blud?) Go out and Pop have to salute new bugs father who hapned to be there but isaacs father only home guard so Pop give him stiff look. molesworth 2 assemble all new bugs and sa he haf 10000 strokes of the kane. Mr trimp sa very like rain tomow.

Oct. 31.

Strong sunshine.

Nov. 1.

Grate consternation rains as deaf master called up for duty at listning post. Mr trimp sa he feel there haf been some mistake. molesworth 2 hope to get shortcake biskit so bring Miss Pringle a dandelion. She sa mother nature about to sleep through winter and think dandlion intresting. Molesworth 2 sa he keen to press it in psalms of the bible about time he opned it. Have wizard game with Peason obbly obbly onker my first conker. Whizz string for record wam and hit deaf master on nut. He give conduc mark to isaacs (throwng stones).

Nov. 2.

Skool pigs birthday. Give presents 3 conkers (baked) dead leafs and mars bar.

Nov. 3.

Skool pig in grate pain.

Nov. 5.

Weedy latin. Mr trimp sa all boys who kno gender rhimes to put up their hand. Don't kno but put up hand as this frequently a good wheeze. Chiz mr Trimp ask me hem-hem but just then mighty air-rade warning all to the shelter dubble. Cheers cheers fuste decent thing the hun haf done. Deaf master give all class conduc mark for going out and fotherington-tomas blub he want to bring in his fairy cycle. Wizard dog fight messershimts crash in hundreds. All clear sound and deaf master dash into shelter he is bats.

Nov. 10.

Gran write and sa vicars wife haf said that children not allowed to canada but she will only belive if she hear from prime minster himself. She do not care what the papers sa.

Nov. 14.

Grate celebrations as Miss pringle and curate to be married hem-hem. Mr trimp make long speech and call on Peason to present skool fish slice. Miss Pringle blush like anything and twist handkercheif. She sa she want us kiddies not to forget our nature lessons and she will give wee prize at end of term for best raffia bag chiz. She is weedy give me merna loy every time. New bugs very affected by miss pringles speech and fotherington-tomas ask her to be mother to him. She sa if very good 5 minites longer before bed and games of oranges lemons. Ugh. 90 boos.

Nov. 15.

Isaacs start making rafia bag.

Nov. 16.

New misteress come instead of miss pringle. Coo she is just like ginger rogers with lipstick and everything. Tell this to matron who sniff and sa she thought her very ordinary girl. She also give me stiff dose of mixture so will not mention agane. molesworth 2 now zoom by he sa he short range bomber and haf shot down skool pig in flames and scored direct hits on valuble objectives on deaf masters trousis. Soon deaf master zoom by to and howls appear. Find molesworth

2 very grave he sa he haf been shot down and he mourning himself. He is bats.

Nov. 18.

Peason come to me he sa terrible thing haf hapned he is in love with new misteress. He is a girly so i slosh him and he slosh me. He is a dirty roter as I haf said pax and sa no fair but he throw blotch pellets at me. All hit deaf master so boo. Find molesworth 2 with hand full of grass blubbing like billyo. He say he burying himself and i sa about time good riddance to bad rubish. fotherington-tomas is chief mute he sa death is very beatiful so tuoogh him up. Isaacs still working on raffia bag he sa to be bigest in the world, in moon in space. He not certain of winning prize as he kno two new bugs working behind closed doors.

Nov. 19.

Gran write she haf called persnally on steamship company and it nonsense no children can go to Canada. She sa mrs Sturgess-green kno two who are acktually there.

Nov. 21.

We haf wizard singing men of Harlack and minstrel boy to the war haf gone. I sing very beatifully it bring tears to my eyes but all sa shut up. Later I see Peason gazing up at new misteress window. He sa will I give her book of Beatiful Thoughts which he haf bagged from fotherington-tomas. He sa go on o you might but deaf master pass with flowers and take new misteress off to Cozy Teashop hot toast yum-

yum. Peason downcast and throw Beatiful Thoughts at isaacs. Mr trimp sa no more air rades after today.

Nov. 22.

Miss latin, weedy french, algy, geog, arith and Eng. owing to sirens.

Nov. 24.

Weedy boy come who swank he haf bomb at bottom of garden. I sa sucks at our home one came whizzing by splosh. Boy sa they dont go splosh they go boom so hard cheddar. Then molesworth 2 spoil it who hapned to be by he sa we haf a 1000 bombs they went like this. He get conduc mark (noise and unruly behaviour). We all sa we votes a bomb which blow up skool but fotherington-tomas blub he sa it is so sad. He will not stop so only votes incendary bombs to burn skool and latin books. Peason then sa what about mr Oates and we are thortful. Isaacs raffia bag now 2 feet long. He thinks he haf a chance for the prize.

Nov. 25.

Deaf master buy sidecar for his moterbike (significant) Tell Peason who sa it better to have loved and lost than never loved anebode and i haf face like a squashed tomato. No bombers toda chiz as I had counted on them and done no prep. Term draws on leafs fall, foopbal matches, rags and toughery. Gran send telegram to sa on no account are we to go to canada as it is not allowed.

Nov. 26.
10000000 secs to Xmas and boo to Germans.

....

Punch, 5 February 1941

ANOTHER SLICE OF MOLESWORTH

Contains: Diary of trimps, chizzes, weeds grandmothers and parots.

Dec. 22.
Term ends with wizard rags. All boys very brave e.g. viz. we leave dorm and walk down mr Trimps stairs in dark. We tell molesowrth 2 buzz off but he come and when half way down he giggle weedily chiz as even deaf master hear who hapned to come by O.K. as he just say God bless you mery boys so we are saved. Pute old cofee walnut in mrs Trimps hat and midnite strike shiver shiver we tremble for fear. Moan groan ghastly green face apear but only matron chiz who blow us up. She sa back to dormtories instanter boys and when we there ghostly cry that curdle our blud but only fotherington-tomas who i haf locked in trunk. Down to study for 6.

Dec. 23.

Home home to gran's cheers cheers. Mrs trimp wave goodbye and cofee walnut still in hat but noone notice as it nestle among grapes and cheries etc. Mr trimp come to station train come in but only weedy tanker (2089763). Mr trimp sa "now we're off" but train do not move then he sa won't be long now but nothing hapen. All boys heads out of windows with ghastly smiles. Mr Trimp sa Afraid it will be some time and train leap out of station. Goodby goodby good ridance bounce on seat, put molesworth 2 in lugage rack and settle back to micky mouse weekly.

Dec. 24.

Xmas eve we haf ripping hammidges katalog I choose aeroplane that will fly six miles absolutely super. molesworth 2 want 1000 soldiers and 3 briagades of dragoons. Mum sa we'll see next year chiz we haf heard that before. Gran add weedily when i was a girl i haf only musical box for xmas. Ermintrude is here agane she still haf her botany book and autograff book with weedy things e.g. cheerio Gwen and by hook or by crook I'll be last in this book. Feeble. She mad on english and read byron (poet) so pull her pigtale but she sa suffering is beatiful. Gran read us Xmas Carol instead of chatterbox but goste is feeble and murdes nobody.

Dec. 25.

Xmas day we wake up early and look at presents ripping chocklate, sweets and sugar plums yum yum.

Xmas day we wake up early and look at presents

Milions of super presents train (mum and Pop) manicure set (gran) Hint? Record parot (Aunt Ciss) Trombone (unckle bingo) and best xmas wishes (isaacs) Unckle bingo is super he cheek gran like anything and call her old girl also rag with us and pretend he monky. He very fond of parot and teach it tuough word. Dinner plum puding and cream I feel i want to burst also crakers which we pull mightily. Haf to kiss ermintrude under misteletoe chiz chiz chiz but see unckle bingo do ditto to parlor maid later which he apear to enjoy. Love?

Dec. 27.

Yar boo british boys are best.

Dec. 29.

Unckle bingo teach us super carol

> Wen sheperds wash their frocks by nite
> All seated round the tub
> a bar of sunshine sope came down
> And they began to scrub.

We think this record funny but ermintrude sa vulgar. She haf weedy frend to stay viz debora parkinson they read feeble books such as the Madcap of the fifth and pam's first term which they sa topping but no blud or tuoughery. Both girls have pash on misteress at skool miss Fish and debora sa that when she pute v.g. on essa she write on Mother nature it the most topping moment of her life. Gosh.

Dec. 30.

Give parot trial flite but he nose dive and crash. Break grans best mug present from baden baden but hide pieces in piano. Careful chizzing.

1941

Jan. 6.

Chiz chiz chiz gran give party with weedy old lades and we haf to peform. Ermintrude recite poem called boots boots boots boots boots all the time and Debora do elves dance but picture relief of ladersmith zoom down from wall. molesworth 2 blub he not allowed to do conjerring tricks on account of puling card out of vicars wifes ear last time but pla faire bells mightily insted. He strike fuste note and bit of mug zoom up and hit ceiling. Gran is peeved she say mug present from m'late husband and of sentimental value chiz as haf german all over. Sent to bed brown bred and water but unckle bingo come in with wizard choc bar.

Jan. 12.

Ermintrude press jerranium in botany book as present for Miss fish. Not bad idea so do the same for deaf master in case he let me off deten. Gran read us chatterbox chiz as boys are all goody goody such as Wee Joe. Shiver moan door open and tuough bear come in but notice parot on back so kno it is only unckle bingo under rug. Think Gran suspeck too as she take down zulu spear from wall and unckle bingo sa ouch. Parot fly through air and land on ernest (dog) and bite ear. All larff hartily xcept ernest (dog) who die for king as usual. Gran sa pretty poll to parot who reply rude word but i think she smile.

Jan. 13.

Do not belive Gran can haf smiled at parots word.

Jan. 15.

Chiz chiz chiz haf to go to dancing class. All boys look like girlies and girls haf weedy bows. Misteress sa feeble things she sa now we are all going to be chickens, little cocks and little hens Tippy toes tippy toes. Moan and groan. molesworth 2 dance mightily and there fat boy called robin but when he being little cock he fall wam. All larff xcept robin's mother who sa i haf tripped him. Chiz as i do not think anebode see. Ermintrude sa dancing misteress is beatiful but not so topping as miss Fish.

Jan. 24.

Moan groan back to skool. Not bad actually as Unckle bingo drive us in his racing car. We go 68 m.p.h. and make rude faces at all policemen. Mr trimp sa to unckle bingo i do not think I haf had the pleasure of meeting you and unckle bingo sa his name is mr scuttlethorpe which is a whoper. Just then he catch sight of new misteress the one like merna loy and give her glad eye chiz as deaf master look daggers. He is sweet on her hem hem. He sa to me what is the meaning of sending me a jerranium and give me conduc mark (insolent behavour). I retort you would not have done that if you were miss fish sir and he agree but probably do not hear.

Jan. 25.

Ha ha ha hee hee hee eleffants nest in a rubarb tree.

Jan. 30.

Tonite we do not haf a bad air rade and wizard bomb drop near skool pig. Mr trimp tell us long story about Great war and leckture us that britain fight for peace and goodwill towards men. He then sit down on draring pin which hapned to be there and give me 6 chiz. See deaf master squeeze new misteress hand. I think he suspeck as he sa he will let me off conduc mark. Chiz parot appear from boot box where i haf hidden him and mr Trimp confiscate him. Do not think parot like it as he sa rude word ten times. Bomb drop and restore peace.

Feb. 1.

Mr trimp go off on important business but see him pute golf clubs in car. Wizard jim lesson with sergent buble's son who swing ninety times on bar and hang upside down from rafter just to show he tuough. Chiz as bottle of BEER drop from pockets just as mr trimp come in agane. Mr trimp sa it will be fine tomow.

Feb. 2.

Sunshine. Gosh.

Punch, 2 July 1941

MOLESWORTH EXCELSIOR

Contains: Diary of tuoughery,
bullys, sloshes, ouches and skool pig.

May 8.

Hols end skool weedy skool chiz. We rub our eyes as it haf been camooflaged but still conspikuous to enemy owing to mrs trimps (headmasters wife) new pink hat. Also enormous new bug who is a tuough and wear long bags (swank). molesworth 2 is a fule and sa you haf face like squashed turnip. He forget to rune away and new bug twist ear slowly. He will present some problems. Charge on big field with criket bat and slosh mightily. Score wizard near miss by skool dog and tuough wam on deaf masters motor bike. Deaf master sa bravo good shot sir so do not think he see.

May 12.

Ferce air rade and wizard bombs drop. Germans all tuough and detmined to extermanate mrs trimps pink hat which important milertary objective. mr. trimp sa Take courage all no danger and all house maids faint including Lily (fat cook). Deaf master apply first ade to cook who scream and sa she never so insulted in her life. molesworth 2 larff like anything (conduc mark — Precocity). Skool pig unhurt but in high nervous condition. Give it bubly gum and chesnut leafs. Mr trimp sa germans make peace any moment; also hitler haf been murded and only an actor in his place.

May 13.

Vilage constable peer over skool hedge.

May 20.

Tuough new bug do not like skool pig he sa pigs poo gosh poo. He buzz conkers at pig but i trip him and he chass me. Hide in rodendron bushes and sa Ya boo swankpot. Unfortunately deaf master hear (miracle?) and give me conduc mark (Tendency to impertnence). Chiz he haf down on me ever since unckle bingo wink at new misteress.

May 24.

Suck up to deaf master. I sa show me how to ride your moter bike sir o you might. He visibly gratified and point out sparking plug. molesworth 2 who hapned to be by sa gosh bet the old grid doesn't go. Deaf master start bike rattle rattle roar roar lamps drop off sparking plugs fly into air and all boys take cover. Mr trimp sa ah a heinkel could tell it anywhere and dash out with a duck rifle. He then fire furously at a wood pigeon he is bats.

June 4.

Pla wizard criket match against staff. Do tuough bowling 90 m.p.h. charge grit teeth ground shakes and all boys tremble. Release ball but only hit skool dog who leap into air and bite new criket coach (long stop) and skool pig chiz. Camooflage skool pig with leafs against new bug, nazis and skool dog.

Release ball but only hit skool dog who leap into air

New bug sneke and I get 6 chiz cruelty to animals. mr trimp sa germans giving eggs to noewegans.

June 8.

Vilage constable lean over bicycle watching skool.

June 10.

Draw wizard face on blackboard but new bug write under drawn by molesworth I chiz. Peason and I decide to tuough him up. Make tuough oath that we will fight in the streets and on the beeches until he is destroyed. Amen. Practise on Isaacs.

June 11.

Decide to tuough new bug up tomow.

June 12.

Decide to tuough new bug up tomow.

June 13.

Decide to tuough new bug up tomow.

June 14.

Argue with Peason who to strike first blow.

Peason sa Fains chiz. Stork new bug stealthily through rodendron bushes but molesworth come up and sa i sa what are you doing lying on ground chiz he is a fule. Crawl further but skool dog bite me in ear. New bug look very tuough but very cunning wait till he not looking then charge. He get me down and Peason just stand by and sa go it he is a funk. After sa to Peason cowardy cowardy custard but postion generally unsatisfactory. Draw wizard invention viz Tankplane on library book.

June 20.

Wizard singing lesson minstrel boy to the war haf gone. All boys sing so beatifully that fotherington-tomas burst into tears. I sa whats up and he reply good thorts ascend like larks chiz he is wonky. Meet new misteress with scent bath poo gosh. Tell matron new misteress loved by all boys: she snort and give me two wopper pills. Coo.

June 21.

fotherington-tomas disappear. Grate confusion and deaf master look at me chiz. All to big skoolroom. fotherington-tomas last seen picking rose and pressing to his heart. molesworth 2 sa he see three bearded men with vilainous xpressions storking him. They all had gats but noone belive him. Then vilage constable apear and all boys cheer as half holday for funeral but super chiz as constable only sa Careless talk costs lives and warn mr Trimp against Rumours. Deaf master find fotherington-tomas on fairy cycle outside PUB (significant?) he sa he going to the war like minstrel boy. Not even kane chiz.

June 24.

New criket coach (long stop) is fussy old man. He make me keep strate bat chiz. He sa he play criket with W.G. and take bat to show me. Bowl tuough donky drop which descend on his nut and all boys congratulate me as no algy or geom for a week cheers cheers. molesworth 2 still sa he saw three men storking fotherington-tomas. I ask him where they go and he sa he sprang upon them and routed them which is a fib. I then sa good thorts ascend like larks and molesworth 2 is stupified. mr trimp declare that we shall beat st. Ethelreds hollow.

June 25.

V. st Ethelreds — lost 10 wkts.

June 29.

Sports weedy sports. Tuough parents arrive and mrs Trimp wear new pink hat. Rune mightily puff puff but always last. New bug swank he win everything chiz but hundred yards Isaacs rune like billyo and beat him holow cheers cheers. Boo to new bug. mrs fotherington-tomas bring air gune. I sa let me haf a go o you might and take wizard pot at mrs trimps new pink hat. Feathers fly in showers cheers cheers. New bug come up who hapned to be by and sa bags and pinch gun but mr trimp arrive incensed about hat and he get 6 cheers cheers cheers cheers cheers. Isaacs blub as he only get criket bat (wally hammond) as prize. He thort the prize was money or he would not haf rune so fast.

June 30.

Criket coach recover consciousness. Deaf master console him and they go off to PUB to hatch plots.

July 1.

Term plod like ploughman. All boys weary of lat french algy conkers matrons and all education. Get tuough deten write out amo, mono rego audio and decide to rune away like fotherington-tomas. Sa goodby to boys in dorm. Peason sa good luck and fotherington-tomas blub quietly. Make cunning rope from sheets like Caveman charlie in boys mag. Goodby goodby noble molesworth. Make super speech from window ledge but fall backwards into cucumber frame chiz moan drone. Boo to everything.

Punch, 6 August 1941

MOLESWORTH MADCAP

Contains: Diary of girls skools, misteresses, beans, girlies, botany books and various chizzes.

July 5.

Mr trimp (headmaster) sa he haf a letter from mum. Tremble tremble as think this probably about vests. But super actually as she sa Pop's regment ordered abroad and we to be near him before he goes. All boys sa chiz lucky dog and deaf master what about deten, amo, mono, rego audio outstanding. Very cunning offer to sa all verbs but only jabber tuough limerick 10 times. Deaf master sa "masterly" and let me off. Pack conkers, jenkins tonsils, dead thrush, 10 may bugs in match box. Farewell, farewell skool pig. Ask tuough new bug if he like a stamp and tread on toe cheers cheers leap into car and away.

July 6.

Haf wizard lunch with mum and Pop viz soup, BEEF and strubres yum yum. Then blow fall. Pop sa that we to go to girls skool nearby and molesworth 2 swoon. Unckle bingo who there too sa he wouldn't half have minded at our age and begin story about barmade but mum sa hush hurriedly. molesworth 2 revive and ask for strubres.

July 7.

A GIRLS skool. Golly.

July 8.

econd blow falls e.g. cousin ermintrude you know the one with the botany book is pupil at skool. Chiz as she is a weed. Mum take us to skool and we meet tuough headmisteress. Mum sa this is nigel and headmisteress mutter gosh and turn away chiz. Go into skoolroom and all girls giggle. They are all feeble and some haf platts, notably ermintrude. All girls then sing skool song

> Rally skoolmates rally
> with crosse and bat and ball
> pla up st. ethelburgas.

Misteress miss parkinson then sa is any little boy ready for his morning milk. I shall never live this down.

July 9.

molesworth 2 is in weedy form called brownies class he sa not bad actually as lesons pappy and all girls are titches. He swank he is a pilot and haf shot down 1,000 heinkels. Small fat girl sa sez you sucks to him. I am in weedy form with ermintrude chiz. All girls swots and proud to kno verbs and all grow weedy beans in flanel. Make tuough experment "What hapnes when 2 pigtales are tied together?" Answer all girls sa beastly beast. They are absolutely feeble.

July 10.

ermintrudes bean sprout two inches long. Weedy

July 11.

No one here to tuough up chiz. All girls haf pash on miss Fish (games misteress) and sa weedy things e.g. I sa joan isn't it ripping i had a simply topping walk beside her in the crock toda. I sa yar boo she haf face like a nanny goat but dora spatchworth (senior pree) report me to headmisteress chiz. Tremble tremble wonder if she haf kane knock knock come in. Headmisteress in chair smoking cig she sa sternly did you sa miss fish haf face like nanny goat.

Did you sa miss fish haf face like nanny goat

Then she larff like anything and sa she rather agree with me and give me wizard piece of toste cheers cheers very butery. She also sa reflectifly: i think you the plainest small boy i haf ever seen. Chiz? Boo to all prees and dora spatchworth.

July 13.

Unckle bingo arrive and get permission for me to keep parot at skool which aunt Ciss gave me for xmas. He sa bird haf now been living for some time in sergents mess and head-misteress look doubtful.

July 14.

Parot see miss fish in jim tunick and utter terrific WORD.

July 17.

molesworth 2 is weedy and muck about with dollies and small girls. I sa do you call yourself a man and he reply ring aring aring aroses poket full of posies tishoo tishoo we all fall down. Ugh. Strike me sideways as parot would sa. Nature study leson on tenis cort. Boo to petals and stamens. Go to sleep with mouth open and miss parkinson sa i can see a little boy who is not listning. molesworth 2 then zoom by followed by little girls. He sa he spitfire patrol so shoot him down. Legs wobble, he clasp head, help help and crash into ermintrudes botany book. Fine specmen of gernanium bished cheers cheers.

July 18.

ermintrudes record bean now six inches long.

July 19.

Peason write me p.c. he haf heard i am at girls skool and ask if i haf been elected most poplar girl. Gosh chiz.

July 20.

Skool pageant absolutely feeble as it called princess and the pixies. Small girls all stand in weedy circle with wings and sing Handsome prince came riding by. Handsome prince is ME chiz but not aloud to galop and haf to skip like girly chiz. As i pass small fat girl she sa come up and see me sometime she is comon. Unckle bingo come and flip bread pellets at ermintrude when she recite. dora spatchworth is Fairy Queen and haf long train but it drag heavily when she enter as molesworth 2 and small fat girl are sitting on it. Miss fish then enter spirit of Pysical Culture. Gosh. Unckle bingo larff so much he haf to go out.

July 22.

Very short of money. Borow ermintrudes bean penny a look but unfortunately parot eat it and ermintrude blub chiz. Miss fish come in and parot sa strike me pink what a dial. Unfortunately she think it me and sa not the way a sir galahad would speak. Punishment am flower monitor for a week chiz. Write stiff letter to peason.

July 24.

Very long crock toda and all girls batey becos miss fish walk with daphne. Girls consider daphne is a weed becos she chew her blotch in prep. Unfortunately 2 tuough boys see molesworth 2 and me and follow crock with tuough words. They sa yar boo yelow knob and we prertend not to notice but despatch quiet stones. Small fat girl sa give em the hot-spot boys but champ champ am powerless. Cheers headmisteress come along and administer wizard blips with umbreller. She is not bad.

July 25.

Haf smoking match with small fat girl. Win by 2 woodbines.

Haf smoking match with small fat girl.

July 26.

ermintrude haf idea she like deanna durbin she bag headmisteress lipstick and muck about with hair. Parot is astounded and peck miss fish cheers cheers. All girls disapprove and write e. hackstall puts on airs in her geom book. Headmisteress sees me in lower fourth passage and sa strike me pink what a dial i think she haf been listning to the parot.

July 28.

Miss fish select me to walk with her in crock. CHEEZ.

July 30.

peech day and unckle bingo is to present prizes gosh. Old lade make long speech and unckle bingo wink at all girls he haf technique. Get weedy consolation prize — mary somers, new girl. Think headmisteress do this on purpose a joke in poor taste. After headmisteress and unckle bingo drink SHERY and molesworth 2 sa that nothing he prefer beer and wine. Small fat girl offer to take him on but he sa he do not feel like it toda.

Aug. 1.

Mum sa pop not to go abroard after all but will guard baracks in wales. Bit of a chiz as we might haf stayed at st. cypranes but that is life. Boo to flower monitors.

Punch, 27 August 1941

MOLESWORTH: MAN OR BEAST?

Contains: Diary of mothers, bording houses, parots, tuough boys and weedy peoply.

August 2.

Sumer hols cheers cheers we leave with mum for seaside. Arive at tuough bording house called mon repos (french) chiz as it is full of old lades including mrs furbelow (prop) and many canares which are not tuough and sing weedily. mrs furbelow look askance at parot which come with us and sa he will be EXTRA including boots baths lights and best sauce yum yum also molesworth 2. Mum sa gosh what a face but mrs furbelow hear and mum prertend she speaking of me chiz.

August 3.

Very tuough bed so wake early. Healthy healthy take deep breaths and whole house tremble 3 old lades leave beds and zoom for air-rade shelter hem hem i don't think. Dash on beach but sea is ten miles out. Cheers as jolly freezing. Also no destroyers or battleships only saucy sue. Read wizard book tarzan of the apes. Determin to be tuough leap on piano and beat chest. Unfortunately mrs baxter (old lade) come in and afterwards eye me closely chiz.

August. 4.

mrs baxter ask mum if i quite as i should be. Mum sa obviously no. chiz.

August 7.

Tuough solders guard beach. molesworth 2 is a silly ass he stroll up to gun and sa bet it doesn't fire. He sa it is an old grid and no more use than a nanny gote. Tuough solder who is an old gentleman and haf red tabs sa indeed and molesworth 2 sa my father is head of army he captain molesworth. Old gentleman sa he will rember name he is only a genral. Tell mum who do not seem pleased. Slide down bannisters with tuough jungle crys.

August 8.

Now i am EXTRA to chiz.

August 10.

molesworth 2 is weedy he buy 2 windmills and zoom about with parot. He sa he twin engine fighter and parot is rear guner. Dive bomb mrs baxters bath chair and parot fall off scoring near miss on parrasoll. molesworth 2 sa bath chair is unlikely to have reached home. Walk along front and meet DEAF MASTER gosh chiz you can never get away from skoolmasters. He visibly shaken to see me but invite me to tea with his old mother adress sea breezes chiz chiz chiz.

August 11.

Tuough tea with deaf master and deaf masters mother who is very ancient. She call him Cecil (n.b. must tell Peason) and give me rock cakes baked with her own hands. She sa Cecil was a lovely baby and when he was 5 he strike nurse gosh tuough. Silence try to eat rock cake crackle crackle bits fly in all directions gigantic raisin narrowly miss dresden sheppherdess. Place rock cake in pocket it will do as a bomb. Deaf master show me buterfly colection weedy unfortunately take out hankerchief (nose) and rock cake fly out badly damaging flertilery.

August 12.

Gun still in same place but still as weedy as all solders pla foopball instead of fighting.

August 14.

Wist Drive at bording house and all old lades very excited they pute on weedy dresses and sa feeble things e.g. clubs are, mrs furbelow. molesworth 2 pla he sa it is pappy and do tuough trumping of partners ace. He sa he trumped trillions of aces in his time he is a swank. Mum is absolutely feeble she haf always to move to the left and mrs baxter swank she haf 53. Mum get booby prize (penny stamp in hat box ha ha) then sa Phew and take stiff drink out of toothmug in bedroom.

Augsut 15.

Rain and haf to stay indoors chiz. Fat lade miss boothroyd aktually read us weedy poem worse than gran's chatterbox e.g. there are faires at the bottom of our garden and rabits stand about and hold the lights. molesworth 2 sa there is a dirty old rubish heap at the bottom of his and miss boothroyd severely browns him off. Alone practice tarzan waddle like goriller and bite cushion with fiendish cries. In middle see mrs baxter looking at me chiz she seem somewhat apprerhensive and grasp parrasoll tightly. Parot (rude bird) sa wot you doing sattiday ma and assault all canares. Parot is tuough.

August 16.

Desine wizard yot with sails from bit of garden seat. At model boat pool it turn over and boy cyril who haf motor boat sneer in konsequence. Challenge him to race and molesworth 2 pute in his toy monky spinach also monkys son as tuough crew. Grate tragerdy bote and monkeys sink also cyril who overbalance in excitement so snubs. Meet deaf master in blazer and white flanels gosh posh. He is with young lade sylvia shriveham soobrette of peerots aktually you know the one who sings weedy songs viz just a song at twilight and no one clap. Walk along prom with them but deaf master do not seem keen on my company.

Augist 17.

molesworth 2 and me are norty e.g. sa boo to mrs baxter. Mum sa she will send us to deaf master for punishment next time. Gosh tuough threat. Good deed we take mrs baxter for airing in bath chair that is i push and molesworth 2 ride in front. Unfortunately wizard spitfire pass and i let go handlebars. Bath chair zoom down slope 240 m.p.h. dogs bark policemen faint bath chair sweep across sands with grate destruction. Moan drone find bath chair stationery in sand castle. molesworth 2 sa absolutely wizard and mrs baxter also enthusiastick she always was one for spills and tumbles. Jolly sporting but do not want another go.

August 18.

Grate activity round gun. Solders move gun up and down then round and round. Genral highly satisfied and solders all go to sleep they are exorsted.

August 20.

Hols end chiz and mum pack trunks. All spades bukets and windmills dispear chiz and we shake sand out of shoes. Canares sing sad songs and parot weep. mrs baxter zoom up in bath chair and give us fruit pastille not bad aktually also deaf master on moter bike. He sa he haf decarbonized bike and she rune smooth as a bird. molesworth 2 sa i don't think and deaf master start bike. Record exlposhon mrs baxter shoot into air and all solders wake and rush to gun. BONK they fire tuoughly and mrs furbelows greenhouse colapse cheers cheers cheers. Boo to jeraniums and zinnerareas.

Punch, 24 September 1941

MOLESWORTH AT GOSTE GRANGE

Contains: Diary of gostes, gnats, shrekes, shudders, grandmothers and wise parots.

August 25.

Mum go off to Pop who is still guarding weedy baracks in wales. Gran take us to tuough creepy house e.g. gorly grange. Chiz as we hopped to go to grans house but this impossible owing to bomb in greenhouse. Gran sa that if it go off she fear she will lose all her glass. She sa she kno we brave little chaps and can stand a shock but all copes of chatterbox haf been also destroyed including 1887–1903. cheers cheers cheers. molesworth 2 sa any hope of ernest (dog) hafing got in the way of something and is stood in korner. (Unfeeling to dum things).

August 26.

Grange is full of tuough serpranos e.g. Secktion of B.B.C. and platoon of dancers from camberwell balet skool who dance weedily. Dancers do fierce dance and tuough lade pla piano mightily. All girls zoom by folowed by M. Anatole at 90 m.p.h. molesworth 2 arive with parot he sa anything up. Parot watch with kritical eye and I expeck rude words as per usual for instance cripes. Aktually both bird and molesworth 2 struck dumb by what they see. Coo,

August 27.

Parot expected shortly to make a statment on the dancing.

August 28.

Gran haf weedy bycycle (non-racing) and ernest (dog) swank becos he haf a basket on handelbars. Chiz as he get uppish and do tuough growling at parot, blakbirds, messerchimts and mr cheese of B.B.C. Absolute swanking as he couldn't hurt a flea. Gran arive from town highly delited she haf found a wizard book for reading instead of chatterbox e.g. Wee tim and tiny Nelly, a book for young peoply chiz chiz chiz. Book is record weedy and stiff with grandmothers chiz. Wee tim pinch an aple and get hell knocked out of him.

August 29.

Gran give weedy tea party and mr cheese come he wear yelow jersey and swank like anything viz here is a rock cake and this is john cheese eating it. He sa ernest (dog) intresting specmen of the highly bred poodle. Chiz as ernest swell with pride and leap at parot. Mr cheese look at parot and sa ah pscitacus arithacus or something and parot is dumb. Strange.

August 30.

No statement from parot about dancing. His lips are sealed.

August 31.

Grate treat mr cheese sa we can come to tuough broadcast to amerika. He ask gran too but she sa why for goodness sake when she can hear it perfeckly well on her own small portable. Exit cheese bafled. Manage to do tuough smugling of parot into broadcast which record weedy viz all sa can you hear me tony this is mum and dad and burst out blubbling chiz. mr cheese then sa we haf in the studio a little british boy and he is going to give a boys message to his brothers over sees. Unfortunately parot then give record hicup (Indigeston that new seed) chiz but mr cheese sa hah ha ha a funny incident and give me trecherous blip. He then ask molesworth 2 to speke (sap). Not bad aktually as he sa cheeky things e.g. all boys in amerika are girlies and describe a 1000000 bombs he haf personaly endured.

September 1.
Balet skool give weedy concert in aid of solders socks.

All girls leap out of shrubery

All girls leap out of shrubery also M. Anatole who now zoom at increased speed 250 m.p.h. All clap and he zoom back agane. All girls then die cheers cheers cheers but come alive agane chiz. Parot still sa nothing but peck ernest (dog) who die for king weedily. Sudenly in come fat fairy cheers cheers as it is UNCKLE BINGO. Ernest yap, boys cheer, parot alite gracefully on mr cheese. Gran also highly delited but audience shout shame shame shame chiz also mr cheese who go tsstss like bycycle pump. M. Anatole faint and is carred off by 5 girls. Gosh tuough.

September 2.

Parot so pleased to see Unckle Bingo he let out record WORD. molesworth 2 highly delited he repeat it fifty times and beat his chest. Unfortunately gran hear also tuough lade mrs gribble who hapned to be cramming buns (N.b. all old lades choose the buns boys want becos they get in fuste) Gran sa to molesworth 2 how can you be such a bad little boy as to sa such a rude THING but molesworth 2 sa its only the one mum uses when she she loses her lipstick. He sa gosh would you like to hear a real WORD you kno that one that Pop uses and is sent out of room. Gran severely browns off Unckle bingo (bad example by larffing).

September 3.

Wee tim has smaked Puss. (Chap 2.) Gosh tuough.

September 4.

Chap 3. Puss has scatched wee tim cheers cheers cheers.

September 5.

Unckle bingo sa haf we ever seen a goste and molesworth 2 sa he haf seen trillions he is a swankpot. Unckle bingo then sa how about a goste tonite and molesworth 2 sa he is not quite feeling like it. Tuough tuough i sa i will come. Midnight strike shiver shiver we creep into unknown haunted room shiver moan drone. Footsteps come chains rattle I draw deep breath it is the maniak fiend the green faced murderer of hounsditch i sa and unckle bingo sa shut up for goodness sake and dive under bed (windy). i join him tremble tremble but lights go on cheers cheers it is only mrs gribble. Tell unckle Bingo who sa he would rather haf green-faced murderer of hounsditch. Chiz as he then pull me out and tell mrs gribble he haf been looking for me all over the house. Super chiz as mrs gribble insist i haf 6 with bedroom sliper. Unckle bingo give me woodbine after but I feel fate haf been hard. Also bedroom sliper.

September 6.

Find parot in holly bush who stare sombrely at balet dancers.

September 7.

Gran give triffric TEA on lawn in honour of old skool friend lady cobblestone. Unckle bingo sa this is the tea to end teas and never was so much eaten so quickly by so few. Looking at me chiz as hadn't properly started. Flies zoom, wasps dive squadrons of gnats atack in formation. Gran and lady cobblestone sa weedy things e.g. fidlesticks prissila cobblestone and all ask mr cheese to recite chiz chiz chiz chiz. All insecks resent poem especially gnats they hammer mr cheese relentlessly. In midle tuough german appear with parashoot all scream but only unckle bingo becos there is a parot on shoulder cracking seed. Gran tell lady cobblestone who score wizard wam on him with cream bun and near miss with ecalir cheers cheers cheers. All larff except mr cheese who dash away and is ringing church bell until old lade appear with prayer book.

September 8.

Parot at last make uterance on balet dancing. He sa what tempo and peck ernest (dog) who leap into basket on handelbars.

September 9.

Dogs and parots haf faces like carots (oficial) Boo to everbode.

Dogs and parots haf faces like carots

Punch, 22 October 1941

MOLESWORTH OF RED GULCH

Contains: Diary of trimps, weeds, tuoughs, coyotes, pintos, sloshes, wams and bonks.

Sept. 12.

Mum haf letter with mr trimp (headmasters) weedy scrawl and she sa gosh. molesworth 2 sa splosh tosh posh and get browned off (2 lines copybook i.e. rat a specis of rodent). Mum then anounce NEWS St. Cypranes haf been BOMBED cheers cheers cheers we faint with joy. mr trimp mrs trimp and skool pig all safe but luftvaff haf established scendency in the air over mrs trimps pink hat and given it severe hamering hem-hem. molesworth 2 sa how about another ten weeks at the seaside mater and coolect another line (bat: cat: sat: mat). Mum sa she broke as a coot and don't kno what your father will sa. molesworth 2 sa he jolly well does and supply WORD to which parot sa amen devoutly. (a roling stone gathers no moss.)

Sept. 13.

molesworth 2 sa Ha here for another two months mater and Mum is thortful chiz.

Sept. 15.

Blow fall mr trimp write to sa "St. Cypranes carries on." Skool will join another skool i.e. st guthrums chiz chiz chiz. molesworth 2 promptly faint and do not revive until mum rustle toofee papers. Tears now come to mums eyes she sa you're going to leaf me after all. Women. Gosh. Now we haf TWO headmasters. Am overwelmed at this thort.

Sept. 20.

Begning of term chiz. New skool is dark and weedy place and all boys feeble e.g. they sing 1 2 3 4 5 6 and ½ boomwalla boomwalla geesewalla geesewalla st guthrums hurray and i am amazed. Very tuough boy approach and sa uh-huh so youse a dude tenderfoot huh. Very peculiar. Boy then sa he lonehand jack boss of Box-R and molesworth 2 sa if you ask him he nothing but a grate big stiff. Boy produce gat and go weehee weehee (bulets). he is bats.

Sept. 21.

Haf come to conclusion boy must haf been playing cowboys.

Sept. 24.

New skool is absolutely weedy it fall to pieces. Drane-pipes crash and tiles drop like leafs. At breakfast mr trimp sa he feel he should bring to mr dashwood (st. guthrums headmaster) that bathroom ceiling coolapsed. mr dashwood roar with larfter and sa he will get the gardner to see what he can do about it. Tuough boy come up to me very mysterous and point out boy in spectackles (swot). He sa beware that guy stranger he comes from the bad lands so i show him fotherington-tomas who zoom by at 90 m.p.h. on fairy-cycle and sa he the ratlesnake, noted bandit. Tuough boy wring hand. (gratitude). Phew.

Sept. 25.

Wizard slide down bannisters but unfortunately seem to nock off big wooden ball at the end. Can't stick it back so determin to hide ball.

Sept. 26.

fotherington-tomas go hoppity skippity weedily and when he pla in goal at foopball he like to pick pritty grass or read book of Beatiful Thorts. He is a girly. Tuough boy go up to him and sa it ain't healthy for you in these parts ratlesnake you cur and fotherington-tomas sa Kind thorts breed kind words and skip away. Tuough boy plainly puzled. Wizard arith with mr dashwood 22 X 2 absolutely pappy easy as pie. No marks as mr dashwood haf mislaid his answer book.

Sept. 28.

Fail to do french prep owing to drawing wizard spitfire on blotch so pop up to matron. i sa i am felling sort of wuzzy. Chiz as it is st. guthrums matron and she is super tuough. She slap me on back and i wizz across room bonk. Saved aktually becos molesworth 2 appere reeling he sa where am i. Also he crib about being wuzzy chiz as he only do not want his plarstercene leson. Decide to scram and own up about french (honesty is the best polercy).

Sept. 29.

Take wood ball out of locker and hide carefully in rock garden. Chiz as tuough boy appere with ball and sa he kinda fancy it is mine. i sa thanks most awfuly and he give record smile chiz. Deaf master now zoom by and admire ball which he sa interesting. Tuough boy leap into air and muck about he sa deaf master is a fine head of steer. He is off his onion.

Sept. 30.

All boys highly delited to hear wizard near miss during geom but only bit of gutter which fall into plaground. mr dashwood sa gardner will look after it and jolly funny if it had been in break and hit one of us on the nut.

Oct. 1.

Peason haf super new rhime viz i went to the pictures tomow and took a front seat at the back. Aktually it is hol toda owing to spectakles boy (swot) getting skol but tuough boy sa this is only a blind to disguise his nefarous business. All boys leap into woods and we track swot. He hold heart and sa poetry i.e. she should have died yestureday creeps in the sylable of such a day. Tuough boy about to pump him full of lead when fotherington-tomas appere. Tuough boy ask him is it a four-footer whose tootin but fotherington-tomas only sa boo you sossage and give him great big push.

Oct. 2.

Hide ball in woodshed.

Oct. 3.

Find ball in locker with note which read Present from box-R. i mean to sa dash it all. 100000000 chizzes.

Oct. 4.

Big boxing competion and everbode slosh everbode. Skool gardner is referee also flap towels and sponge blud. mr dashwood highly delited he sa straight left sir gad a lilly and drawn blud but mr trimp do not think this make good impreshon on parents. Wizard bun fight after mr trimp hand cakes very perlite he sa do try a pink one. Aktually mr dashwood spoil everthing he sa haf a snifter trimp old boy and i kno your missus likes a quiet one occasionaly. Large pikture Releaf of ladysmith then crash to ground and gardner is sent for.

Oct. 6.

Chiz all is discovered. mr trimp sa any boy who kno anything of ball from bannisters to own up. i am about to pute up hand when tuough boy leap to feet and sa it was him. Highly delited but grate sacrifice i sa please sir it was me. Chiz as noone belive me. Tuough boy is let off and i get conduc mark (untruthfulness).

Oct. 7.

molesworth 2 go to matron he sa he haf terrible sore throte and how about a blackcurrent lozenje yum yum. Matron sa no and what about your wire you kno the one that keeps his teeth straight. molesworth 2 sa choke that blatt and rune away. matron very ratty and give record pink powders.

Oct. 8.

Hurra for all boys.

....

Punch, 10 December 1941

MOLESWORTH THE FASHIONPLATE

Contains: Diary of toffs, swanks, swizzes, bishes, bonks, plus fores and various bits of HARD CHEDDAR.

Nov. 12.

St. Cypranes is still at st. guthrums you kno where we moved after tuough bombing of all latin books. All record weeds are still here i.e. mr trimp (headmaster) mrs trimp deaf master molesworth 2 and tuough boy who is bats he thinks he super cowboy RED NED. Also super weed five star selexion mr dashwood (st. guthrums headmaster) chiz chiz chiz. Toda is memorable as absolute new bug arive. We are doing weedy french with deaf master who sa get on with next exercise rats do not love cats. Peason sa gorblimey why should they (conduc mark "slang") when sudenly door open. Grate confusion as deaf master hide newspaper and all boys remove penknives dinky toys and liberry books with utmost speed. mr trimp then reveal record BOY who is jolly old he is 14 and wear plus fores gosh. mr trimp sa cold snap will brake tomow.

Nov. 13.

Ice in all toothmugs.

Nov. 14.

molesworth 2 see record new bugs plus fores he is amazed and dive bomb them mightily. New bug do not get ratty he sa molesworth 2 is a mere tick cheers cheers cheers he haf hit the nail on the head. All juniors and weeds of plarstercene class are also amazed at plus fores and folow new bug sucking thumbs weedily. I dercide to tuough them up and charge full tilt but they are record weedy chiz they larff like girlies and when i chass them they sa boo sossage from behind trees chiz. fotherington-tomas aktually pedal up on fairy-cycle and sa beast. Maybe i am losing my grip.

Nov. 15.

New bug appere with green pork pie hat. Gosh.

Nov. 16.

Pork pie hat draw record crowds all plarstercene class also tuough cowboy who is amazed. He sa pard that lid look plum loco to me but then see 3 rooks and rune away. He sa rooks are trailing him he is bats but what can you expect with a name like cecil winkle. molesworth 2 now zoom up and sa gosh what a hat (tact) but everone else haf good manners and only stare with mouths open.

Nov. 17.

st guthrums still wonky and woobly and chimbly pots crash mightily all day. Toda there is special dancing class chiz chiz chiz weedy old gcyser drive up in cranky old grid and make us do weedy things i.e. i haf to rumba with fotherington-tomas chiz chiz chiz. Old geyser leap mightily and mr dashwood stroke moustash thortfully he sa not bad eh trimp old boy, gad what a chassis etc. Geyser then do super leap floors tremble house shuders and pikture releaf of ladysmith zoom to ground bonk. molesworth 2 then offer to pla his famous piece faire bells on piano and i order all boys to shelter as this far more dangerous than bomb. Fortunately tea bell ring and he zoom away at 200 m.p.h.

Nov. 18.

Speak to record new bug he sa dancing not a bad show but persnally he simply adored good swing, jive or jiterbug. He sa he haf simply marvelous evening at savoy in the vac and molesworth 2 sa crikey fancy dancing with girls gosh. New bug sa certainly and molesworth 2 repli coo what a woper and rune away with pork pie hat. See tuough cowboy slinking among trees the rooks are still hounding him.

Nov. 19.

Boy with spektacles you kno the swot who got the skol approche mr dashwood in break with folowing on piece of paper e.g. (a–b) x (y–z) but mr dashwood sa he haf not time now he will give answer tomow.

Nov. 20.

mr dashwood deep in thort. He seem worred.

Nov. 21.

Highly delicate situation arise toda as we haf weedy crocodile with deaf master and meet super local tuough boy dirty pete famous for gang of oiks. Deaf master see gang at end of road and talk sudenly with deep interest about robin redbreasts chiz he haf not forgoten vilage tuough who shout garn big boots and thro walnut at him. Aktually dirty pete see famous pork pie hat and is dumbfounded until peason make long nose (rude). Tuough voley of stones folow also WORDS and they sa feeble things e.g. ladeeda cecil and yar frankenstein. Cheers cheers new bug leave crock and deal dirty pete wizard wam on snitch and all better boys join super scrap with blows and curses. fotherington-tomas then skip up weedily and sa to er is human to forgive divine which he get from book of Beatiful Thorts but he only get wam and rune away blubing also dirty pete cheers cheers he blub he will tell his ma. Deaf master still talk to swot about redbreasts and feeble little creatures of nature but think he must haf noticed.

Nov. 22.

wot catch mr dashwood who sneke through algy answer book he is still thortful.

Nov. 23.

Decide to be SWANK like new bug.

Nov. 24.

molesworth 2 zoom up he sa he is an ariel dog fight but he is gnerous he will let me be messerschimt 109F as long as i promise honour bright to haf blak smoke poring from port engine and becom lost to view beneathe clowds. i sa absolutely no fains twice as i haf dercided to become a swank. molesworth 2 sa don't care so boo and shoot down matron skool gardner 5 new bugs and robin in flames and return safely to his base (dog kenel). Absolutely drift up to sick room and sa what ho mato how about puttin a monogram on my vests my dear but she only take temperature and give me white powder. Nuisance. Also make rude remarks about vests i.e. they are not fit for beste of field to wear. i repli molesworth 2 haf got to haf a crack at them yet and with this riposte ooze down to coco and biskits.

Nov. 25.

Rooks still trailing tuough cowboy he sa the net is drawing in.

Nov. 26.

French weedy french deaf master ask feeble questions about mama rat but SWANK break rule of class e.g. to sa i dunno sir. He answer in french and deaf master is amazed. SWANK deliver grate thort: Masters are a necessary evil and deaf master give him one mark i do not think his hearing improves. Wizard high tea frizzly sossages all boys guzle absolutely and take record bites especially molesworth 2 who make important statement viz where sossages are concerned i belive in scorched earth policy.

Nov. 28.

mr dashwood sa how about a–b? he is visably disapointed when swot shake head.

Nov. 29.

Continue tuough swanking and absolutely brush hair. Peason sa how about sloshing match but i sa no thanks old man not just at the moment. Unfortunately molesworth 2 hapen to be by on way to steal biskits and he larff like anything. However sa how about another helping of sardines my dear to gerturde (maid) and she aktually bring 3 complete with tails cheers cheers and molesworth 2 is very impressed.

Nov. 30.

Stern lekture from mr trimp becos all skool call gerturde my dear.

Dec. 1.

Rooks are closing in on cowboy.

Dec. 2.

Find tuough cowboy lying on floor in big skool his eyes are closed. He sa come closer molesworth they got me take this and give me 3 dinky toys. He then expire until Peason go by with compass then come to life agane. He then want dinky toys back chiz that is the way of the world. SWANK sa i simply must come and sta with his pater in the vac or would it bore me to tears. Can't help it the beste come out in me and i sa yes it jolly well would bore me and call him weedy swankpot. He administer sound blipping and tuoughery but worth it.

Dec. 3.

Swot sa wot about the answer to mr dashwood. mr dashwood sa of course of course a–b x y. When swot shake head mr dashwood give him super blip cheers cheers he haf got the right answer at last.

Dec. 4.

Boo to rooks cowboys swankpots and all boys.

....

Punch, 24 December 1941

MOLESWORTH OF THE REMOVE

Contains: Diary of oiks, headmasters, ow yarouch, crikey and various ungentlemanly cries.

Dec. 8.

st cypranes is still evackuated at st. guthrums and all recod weeds flourish i.e. 2 headmasters, skool dog, matron, deaf master etc. all enemy agents in that order. Toda tuough man arive to see mr trimp (headmaster) with record OIK (son) called cyril who haf close resemblance to dirty pete the vilage tuough. Tuough man sa look here old man how about me sending my nipper to yore place? Herr trimp look down nose (long) he sa "We are full." Tuough man then wink and sa I AM A BUTCHER HOW ABOUT IT NOW and cyril is instantly admited chiz. All boys sa jolly shame and swanky new bug yo kno the one with the pork pie hat sa he must serously consider resigning. All aplaud this except molesworth 2 who sa good ridance to bad rubish and rune away.

Dec. 9.

Gran write p.c. She haf seen a poster which sa go to it and intend to become lady porter. Gosh tuough.

Dec. 10.

French class. Deaf master address oik he sa turner where is papa rat? Oik sa cor stone me how should i kno and go to top of class (flewency and good prunciation). Oik is super weed aktually and always wanting to pla jolly japes on masters. He sa i votes felows we do a merry prank i.e. pute buket of water on classroom door. He gets these idears from comicks he is keen on bob cherry, billy bunter etc. and read about them in prep he will get cobbed one day.

Dec. 11.

Mum write letter about Gran becoming porter. She sa what a wonderful old lade Gran is dedcating herself to the countrys cause. Very sad chiz it bring tears to my eyes i am filled with noble visions. Unfortunately Pop add note "This ought to finish the old geyser off" and i larff synically over poridge.

Dec. 12.

Toda there is weedy pla by plarstercene class chiz. They are all wee bunnies and gnomes. fotherington-tomas jump for joy he is a pixie but molesworth 2 absolutely browned off he is CHIEF GNOME cheers cheers cheers. He is a weed and i sa how about you swanking you are a spitfire pilot when you haf to sa Come elves let us do what we may to help the princess. Pla is record weedy being full of good deeds and noble thorts but OIK do good thing viz he bag Chief Gnomes trousis in interval. mr trimp sa unless trousis are returned imediately pla cannot go on and all boys cheer they do not want to watch it anyway. mr trimp then get batey and sa culpritt to own up or no half hol but swanky new bug point out that what the nazis are doing in paris and get conduc mark (superiority).

Dec. 13.

Matron find Chief Gnomes trousis in my tuck box chiz. She sa she will let matter go no further if I promise not to rage or pilow fight in dormtories. i promise faithfully and she believe me (sap). Swanky new bug sa whole skool seethe with vice and coruption. He sa no beauty anywhere and seem to look at me chiz. Don't care so boo.

Dec. 15.

OIK is absolute weed he is only keen on stink-bombs and weedy ink darts which do not fly and canot do the pappiest sums. Toda we haf algy fuste lesson in afternoon which is the one where mr dashwood (st. guthrums headmaster) always sa get on with xsamples and then go to sleep. Unfortunately he break rule and wake before bell executing wizard pincer movement on OIK with ruler. Oik sa yaroo ouch goshsir i meantersay sir cor sufering snakes and recive second blip which all boys watch with delite. mr dashwood also give him deten although Oik offer him three pork chops and a nice loin of lamb without coupons.

Dec. 17.

Hatch plot with peason to tuough up OIK on account of Chief Gnomes trousis. Oik sa look here you felows you did ought to be reasonable how about three tins of spam and we are inflexible and sa we will tuough him up and haf tins as well. Oik then sa his dad can get us comisions in air force and fotherington-tomas highly excited he wish to be air cadet. molesworth 2 sa gosh you can't even ride your fairy cycle yet and bow 3 times he think he is witty. He then rune off to bomb skool dog and steal blackcurrant lozenges.

Dec. 18.

Gran write she highly disgusted she canot be a porter on account of stationmaster sa he is out of trains and haf none under the counter. Gran declare she strongly suspeck he pull her leg but will make xplosives instead.

Dec. 19.

We haf weedy shepherds pie but mr dashwood tuck into pork chops. Significant?

Dec. 20.

Toda there is jim comp and all boys do tuough things to the manner born we do record figure marching but molesworth 2 is weedy he forget to turn and march into tea room. All boys then hang upside down and pink cakes rane from molesworth 2's jersey he is a guzler. mr dashwood highly excited he dash into midle and sa gad a human pyramid magnificent and throw fotherington-tomas into air. parents screme mr trimp hide eyes but he do not break any bones chiz. Boys then clime on mr dashwood who sa all storms a rugged oak can bare. Wizard crash folow and great aplawse.

Dec. 21.

Hurra for Xmas. Boys go mad in wizard rags and scrag all masters, dive bomb matron, hammer at bases of all latin books and suround skool dog in ring of steel. molesworth 2 is shot down in larder and fail to return to his base. Chiz. Ouch yaroo for Xmas.

Dec. 22.

Good ridance to skool.

1942

Punch, 18 March 1942

MOLESWORTH THE DOG FANCIER

Contains: Diary of dogs, parots, land girls, chizzes, weeds, grandmothers and unckle bingo.

Feb. 19.

we are not at skool cheers cheers i.e. becos molesworth 2 in contack with wizard case of measles it is about time he did something sensible. Grate confusion folow and mum ring up gran who sa she would rather haf a pair of ravening wolves which is what comes of molesworth 2 saing boo to scrooge when she read xmas carol last dec. 24. Pop make helpful sugestions i.e. how about parking us at the savoy hotel or he would dig a large hole for us on wimbeldon co-mon. Mum is not amused and get aunt ciss to take us at her farm you kno where ermintrude (girl) and weedy parot are. molesworth 2 blub he want to live in the hole he is a girly and not tuough at all.

Feb. 20.

Stern pie jaw from mum she sa reason peoply do not like hafing us becos we are not gentlemanly chiz e.g. sir galahad would not haf said "is that all" when gran give him graf spee batle game for birthday. molesworth 2 sa thats nothing you should haf heard what pop say about the mitens she knited. He ask if mum would like to hear the WORD as he haf jotted it down in skoolboy diary 1942. After i sneke about and pop ask mum how did it go but she also utter WORD gosh coo. Rub chest to bring up measle spots but it no go chiz.

Feb. 21.

Gran now making munitions in xplosives factory

Gran now making munitions in xplosives factory. Oficial. Pop sa she canot last more than a week and he will buy bottle of strong wine on the strength of it.

Feb. 22.

Arive at aunt ciss and ermintrude meet us at station chiz. She sa shame nigel molesworth for puting molesworth 2 in lugage rack just becos he will not share micky mouse weekly you are no knight. Our parot the one who was brought up in the sergents mess see ermintrude and sa cor lumme what a dial he is no knight either. Farm is super and folowing dogs in residence i.e. punch smut sweep and geobels. Also ernest (dog) who belong to gran. Bull is still frendly but molesworth 2 swank he haf been bitten by a chicken he is absolutely weedy.

Feb. 23.

Chiz as aunt ciss make us WORK e.g. walk each day and get no sweets, no chocs, no mars bars, no cigs and no soap from vilage shop. Also walk with red flag in front of miss penberthy (land girl) when she drive tractor. Super chiz aktually as i walk all the way into vilage before i find she haf turned into ploughed field. i supose i did look silly but no need for vilage oiks to sa i haf red nose. Aunt ciss parot is still weedy and glad to take cold bath. He sa brrh brrh good to be alive but our parot refuse to get off perch till lunch time and then complane about the seed. Aunt ciss sa he is a worm and a bad sport chiz he has never been the same since he broadcasted you kno the time. he think everbode thort him a nightingale.

Feb. 24.

Pop write that gran still in one piece but only a mater of time. He sa one thing about her working in xplosives factory she will get her wish about being scatered to the 4 winds and no kremation xpenses either.

Feb. 27.

Wizard field marshal arive at farm cheers cheers as it is only UNCKLE BINGO up to his tricks he is bats. He order molesworth 2 to be shot for xceeding points ration and molesworth 2 blub he is frited and unckle bingo haf to ofer him 1939 mars bar so aunt ciss won't hear. He then go to pub and do super things viz he xchange ernest (dog) for pint of BEER and 20 cigs. He tell landlord ernest a fine ratter which is a whoper and molesworth 2 is specheless with admiration.

Feb. 28.

Rat chasses ernest (dog) down hole and unckle bingo haf to buy him back chiz. He ofer to take rat instead but recive stiff refusal.

Mar. 2.

col. threpperton (squire) give weedy dog show in vilage hall and we take all dogs after tuough combing. Dogs are tuough and bite everbode including wilfred postmistress baby which not bad aktually as baby is a weed and keep throwing pink rabit out of pram what is the sense of it. molesworth 2 swank he is a dog chiz he only do it to get a biskit. Aunt ciss give 6 to 4 on punch for long begging competion but chiz as no dog will stop except ernest who can only die for the king anyway and he is awarded prize. col. threpperton present prizes i.e. threpperton bowl and enormous dog bound up bow 3 times and shake him by the hand. Cheers cheers dog is only UNCKLE BINGO and he swank his name champion duff of throgmorton but noone belive him. col. threpperton sa he should be drummed from his regment but all dogs highly delited and all bite each other.

Mar. 4.

Dogs exorsted they canot carry out national service i.e. guard petrol dump while sergent talk to miss penberthy. Only ernest (dog) report for duty he would wet or fine and do not pretend he haf a sore throat. They will give him a pike next.

Mar. 5.

Pop write p.c. that gran haf no chance of xploding now as she haf row with forewoman who do not think it wise to haf primus stove in filling shed tea or no tea.

Mar. 6.

Buzz wizard brick at army oficer with red cap chiz as i think it unckle bingo and i haf to do bunk from british army. Oficer complane to aunt Ciss but she sa i am sure nigel is the last boy to throw stone and wink heavily she is jolly decent. She ofer oficer cup of tea but miss penberthy come in and he take one look and sa he must be getting on.

Mar. 7.

Days wear on dogs bulls chickens and land girls haf shoulders to wheel. ermintrude sa always darkest before dawn but i am browned off i shall be in the army soon. Decide to run away to skool. GOSH.

Mar. 8.
Chiz and this wilfred molesworth saing it.

....

Punch, 20 May 1942

MOLESWORTH AND THE DOMESTIC PROBLEM

Contains: Diary of grandmothers, chars, pies, cups of fresh, cooks and various weeds.

April 17.
Skool break up late chiz owing to spring sowing in mr trimp's allotment and all boys help. No rags or scrambles chiz as mr trimp (headmaster) give tuough pijaw on austerity. He sa all boys to help parents in difficult times viz do little things in home chiz chiz he must be potty. All boys are browned off at this except fotherington-tomas who highly delited he sa he hope to do BIG things and will bring his mummy posies of daffs and sho willing spirit he is a grate girly and likes dollies. molesworth 2 sa it won't be so bad as he bags cook breakfast which is tuough on the bacon he will eat it all. Overhear deaf master who sa whoopee end of term and buzz latin book secretly at matron. Can he be human?

April. 18.

Same old story we go to grans for hols chiz as she jolly tuough and sa maners makyth manne e.g. molesworth 2 not to twizzle knife on table at dinner. Don't blame her acktually becos molesworth 2 sa Who is biggest fool in world? and knife point to her. We wish butler was here he would haf enjoyed it as ushual but he now in R.A.F. (weehee bonk) also housemaid and all maids. Gran sa she only hope mabel drop as many bombs on germany as she did plates in kitchen and we will win war. ernest (dog) think this funny and bark furously he is a weed and gets no better.

April 18–28.

Think about doing little things in home.

April 29.

Determin to HELP in home.

April 29.

Was i wise in this decission?

May 5.

Make up mind. Rise early to make bed but dercid to do later also clean teeth and brush hair. Find mrs winkle (new cook) in kitchen with wizard frizzly smell. i hope to cash in on smell but chiz as it only what the hens haf. mrs winkle highly delited i clean shoes and make wizard joke e.g. too many cooks muck the soup at which she larff hartily. Also she haf daughter (gladys) who do all work and is super sneke she sa oo mum that little boy clening blak boots with the brown chery blossom. Chiz but mrs winkle only larff and pour huge cup of tea also smoke cig. She sa gladys win embroidery prize at orchard road skool and i repli i can well belive it and exit, master of the situation, to buzz morning bricks at tin roof.

May 6.

Gran is peeved i.e. becos she doing nothing to help old country in hour of peril. She sa if invasion come she do not intend to sta put. All her life she haf never stayed put and she will not start now. She sa when hour strikes she will be out there scorching the earth and all her friends are impressed and drop tuough stitches. molesworth 2 swank he will be a quisling and boo to everbode he is browned off becos only one slice of the ginger for tea.

May 7.

Gran sa she haf such nice letter from mrs fotherington-tomas and david being a perfect little angel in house. Too early to make statement on this communique.

May 8.

Dercid to help agane with shoes etc. Find mrs winkle who lie on sofa with cig reading racing and football news while gladys do all work e.g. she scrub floor and sa oo mum is it not good to be working she is like wee nell in chatterbox. Start tuough clening of all shoes but chiz as molesworth 2 come in he is afraid i am at bacon or other food. molesworth 2 sa let me help you o you might and when i tell him to buzz off he sa fool and i sa million fools. mrs winkle highly

Gran is peeved…She sa when hour strikes
she will be out there scorching the earth

delited she sa kick him in the stumick like the wrestlers do but gladys sa i don't fite or sa harsh words do i mum she is a weed. Dercid to tuough up molesworth 2 but he smell chicken food and zoom away to cheat hens. gladys sa each temptation resisted is feather in an angel's wing and mrs winkle is amazed.

May 10.

Find text on pillow. He who refranes is thrice blest. Who can haf done this?

May 11.

Gran take us to weedy concert at happy home canteen chiz chiz chiz as she sa i am to do famous imitation of hitler. i sa no dash it all but gran repli imitation is super and admired by all who haf seen it gosh am i that good? All soldiers browned off at thort of concert they eat sossgaes dejectedly. Start off fercely shake fists moostash tremble all hairs stand on end but chiz as i friten baby in second row also come to JOKE but noone larff until moostash drop off chiz then pandermonium and all cheer. molesworth 2 blub he haf not been asked to pla faire bells on piano and all soldiers agane sunk in misery. molesworth 2 begin to pla mightily sossages fly into air mashed potatoes leap like pancakes ham sanwiches fly apart and soldiers deeply impressed it is like the noise of battle. Gran leave note that she unable to make final speech. Also she doubt whether anyone else will be able if molesworth 2 pla faire bells anything like he ushually do.

May 12.

Find next text on toothmug whiteness is the coat of love. Whose is this poison pen?

May 14.

Back to kitchen for work and find mrs winkle with cup of tea and gladys who blak grate delitedly. Also molesworth 2 who very grim as he making woolton pie. gladys sa oo mum just look at what the little boy is doing but mrs winkle sa son't fret she glad to see him enjoying his tiny self cheers cheers cheers she haf hit the nail on the head. molesworth 2 cook mightily pie buble and tremble pastry sizzle flames lick hungrily and all are delited gosh wizard. mrs winkle sa a teaspoon of treacle would burn up nice she is in fits she can hardly drink her tea on account of it being a whole week's wasted.

May 15.

Overhere gran who tell frend that mrs winkle a good little worker. Coo.

May 16.

Sun shine hurra fror criket and blossoms of nature. Everbode is feeble and weedy for evermore. Aim crokey ball at ernest (dog) make gran applepie sa boo to mrs winkle and pute molesworth 2 in hen food becos he swank he is a chicken. Only gladys remane. Give her wizard text viz girls are feeble and she so shocked she will not speke to me and peace descends.

May 17.
Tra-la for the sumer and birds nesting.

....

Punch, 29 July 1942

MOLESWORTH'S JOLLIEST TERM

Contains: More girls skools, flower monitors, prees, tuoughery, headmisteresses and fruit,

July 6.
Mum arive at st. cypranes cheers cheers she bring us wizard SWEETS inkluding whipped cream wallnuts. Chiz as molesworth 2 is suspious viz he sa Are not these the walnuts laid down for Armistice night? Mum blush chiz and blow fall i.e. Pop on embarkation leave agane and we to go to st. ethelburgas (girls skool) gosh chiz. mr Trimp (headmaster) sa i am loss to eleven: chiz feel he is insincer as last match i make duck, blow 8 wides and stun long stop. Tell peason i am finishing term at eton to get feel of it. This is fib but molesworth 2 come by and swank he is a girl so cat is out of bag. Sell all dead maybugs at controlled price.

July 7.

Find large DOLLY on bed chiz. Strongly suspeck deaf master who wink heavily at matron over korn flakes. No normal man would do this unless plotting. Hope to sneak away in skool taxi but alas all boys yell yar boo doris, farewell sno white ect. chiz and peason sa he haf always been struck by my beauty. Funny? mr Trimp sa Order order do not rag them, fellows and all stop except deaf master who ask to be my valentine and skip weedily in front of taxi. i do not think he can haf heard.

July 8.

Definite boos to all girls.

July 9.

First day. Tuough headmisteress take one look at me and mutter gosh what i will do for money. Weedy bell go tinkle-tinkle: all girls, prees, flower monitors and other weeds asemble for Morning Meeting viz singing skool song and tuough gigling. This is big morning aktually as miss fish (games misteress) haf leaped higher over horse than any other games misteress in england and win prize. Feeble feeble dora spatchworth (senior pree) sa Come on, st ethelburgas, lets give our heroine skool yell. All weeds than sa as follows: Q. Whats the mater with miss fish? A. she's all right. Q. Whos all right? A. miss fish is all right. Consider this perfecktly feeble so do headmisteress who pat all girls on head including dora spatchworth who she pat rather harder than necessery. She haf right idears.

July 10.

Q. What's the mater with molesworth 1? A. he is entirely browned off.

July 12.

Day dawn fine and bright chiz it is morning of tuough match v. st. cynthias. All girls haf but one topick viz outcome of this grate game. They sa Won't it be spiffing if spatchworth caries her bat? Bat is so big aktually that it is miracle if anyone can carry it and i sa so fearlessly i am even more browned off i.e. becos am in Wren patrol and haf to cry Chirup-chirup if in difculty or catching spy. Tuough team arive but super chiz as dora spatchworth bowl them all out. Headmisteress sa you can't help taking wickets with a face like that and rap girl smartly with sunshade who sa d. spatchworth is the top. Will st. ethelburgas do it? molesworth 2 sa as a mater of fact he do not care brass button one way or the other and buzz small stone at miss fish. No prep on account of winning match and regret to state pla tuough game of tag. Gosh.

July 14.

Peason write letter. He sa his admiration haf turned to something deeper and write poem viz

Hearts afire, hearts so true
betty darling i love you.

A joke in poor taste.

July 16.

Small fat girl is still at skool you kno the one who is tuough and chew pen, scratch head also carve beta thomson is soppy on desk. She wish to let us in on RASBERRY RACKET viz pinch rasberries from skool garden and sell to ma timmis (pakenham gardens produce of the soil, Ltd.) Chiz rember all sermons, pijaws, kanes and shake head. molesworth 2 sa why not guzzle rasberries gosh? In the end give fruits as present to skool staff with compliments. Top in scripture. Significant?

July 17.
molesworth 2 zoom by with trowel. He swank he is digging for defeat and all small girls are impressed.

July 18.
Anual Pagaent. All girls pute on white dresses and tuough headmisteress haf new hat she stare in mirror and is aghast at what she sees. Pagaent begin viz HUMAN WHIST we are all feeble cards and haf to skip weedily chiz. molesworth 2 swank he is two of clubs cheers cheers he get dealt into wrong hand and trump dora spatchworth (ace of hearts). Small fat girl suggest we bag bunch of grapes from headmisteress hat as would never be missed among so much fruit but i refuse. Hand round ices i.e. molsworth 2 sa May i tempt you to an icecream, molesworth 1? and i repli allow me to press you to one of mine. Do 9 strawberry 3 vanilla affect boys?

July 19.
Yes.

July 21. Pop's embarkation agane cancelled and he is to sit in barn near bognor and give all solders fatigues chiz.

No real sign of end of term hols bombs or more rasberries. Weedy weedy all girls swot, bees place long noses in flowers and birds sing feeble songs. Buzz criket ball at dora spatchworth, brick at blakbird and small pellet at miss fish. All miss. That is life.

July 22.

Chirup-chirup and boo to von bock.

....

Punch, 21 October 1942

MOLESWORTH GOES RUSTIC

Contains: Diary of harvesting, loonies,
aples cows seeds farmers and fruit.

Aug. 28.

i sa gosh all plans upset i.e. Pop should not haf been on embarkation leave at all as war ofice were thinking of molesworth c St. J. A, major, r. sigs who haf already been in egypt two years. Pop sa it is scandalous disgraceful but later see him do hornpipe in bathroom and sa 8 weeks leave in bag and no foreign service hurra cheers cheers. Mum also do hornpipe but brake plate which will haf to be replaced as on inventory and not one she hat sneaked trom locked cupbord. Situation leave molesworth 2 cold. He sa he haf long suspeckted impasse at the ministry and zoom away to inspeck plum harvest.

Aug. 29.

molesworth 2 confined to bed. Plum harvest rather bakward (oficial).

Sept. 1.

Complications viz Pop haf choice of joining unit in aberdeen or stationed next door to grans house. He dercid immediately for aberdeen and buzz small cherry stone at molesworth 2 who sa So you can't take it? from larder. Mum is browned off at this i.e. becos Pop always so nasty about mother but find 2 unladered stokings and ½ botle of scent poo gosh and cheer up at once. P.C. arive from gran who sa she going to the country to fite on harvest front and think boys should do bit also. Strong pi-jaw from Pop who sa all boys to help national effort and bend backs with will. Chiz as he sa to mum Now we can haf wizard last week in town. Hay-ho all boys are stooges.

Sept. 4.

Cheers cheers arive with gran at tuough farm viz golightly court farm dainty teas cream camping ground plums in season. Cow chikens dog pig ect see gran and cry bitterly. Knock knock where is farmer? Enter super weed viz silas croker (farmer) he see gran and almost moo too. Eat tuough tea in parlor but chiz as molesworth 2 sa tea O.K. but what about cream plums and camping? All larff inkluding mrs croker, granny croker and granny croker's friend mrs posnett they sa molesworth 2 such a pritty child cheers cheers. All then look at me and words freeze on lips wot do they expect robert taylor?

Sept. 5.

Chirup chirup rise with dawn but all animals sleeping chiz but not bad aktually as zoom through wood and pester all flies wasps and bluebotles. Return to farm which in confusion as dairy haf not called. Gran sa why not milk own cows but nothing doing as only one cow i.e. Poppy which haf not given milk for 3 years. silas croker sa he slowly coming to conklusion that cow no use. Gran then sugest slorter house but mrs posnett fante away she canot stand blud. molesworth 2 highly delited he swank blud daggers ect favorite subjeckts and granny croker fante too. Result 2 heavy bombers down. Pilot, molesworth 2 award himself v.c.

Sept. 8.

Heavy rane storm. silas croker shake head.

Sept. 9.

Thunder and hail. Croker in despair.

Sept. 10.

More rane. Croker sa if this do not hold up he will be ruined. Gran leap to feet. She sa give her a rake and harvest will yet be saved. molesworth 2 agree, providing there sunshine and light drying wind and ooze off to bomb chikens out of drawing room. Gran now return to parlor with rake but croker repli no go as no harvest anyway. He only worried becos he haf left mack in vilage bus and canot do rounds for insurance coy. He ask if he can intrest gran in lfe policy or burglary risk. Find molesworth 2 who lie in dog kenel he haf been shot down by chiken and is dead once more.

Sept. 11.

Gran find PROSPECTUS in bedroom viz. nice quiet little company with firm divdends invest now.

Sept. 14.

Take farm dog for hunt but feeble aktually as dog think he frend of man and only wish to pla with rabits like christofer robin, poo and wendy. Pop into vilage for 2 oz. persnal rash-ion but meet Loony lil, vilage idiot, in honeysukle lane she is bats and sing feeble songs viz: Maying lads tie on your ribons and wheel empty pram what is the sense of it? Chiz aktually as she sa i am long lost son. Vilage oiks highly delit-ed they cheer like mad so tuough up young george thomas also postman baines youngest. From all these operations two of our teeth are missing.

Sept. 15.

croker ask gran if she haf ever studied comercial aspekt of mushroms?

Sept. 16.

Poppy (cow) go too far as she drink all milk rashion. Gran sa if not slorter house why not market? mr croker agree and borow traler from a.r.p. He haf only paid for half of Poppy but will raise rest on sale and that will make her all his. Auctioneer sa what am i bid for this remarkable beast and molesworth 2 swank as he think he refering to him. Make tuough repli i.e. i would not give d. for anyone who haf been shot down by chiken he is a fule. Farmers all shake heads at Poppy but cunning cunning croker run up bidding and finally buy for twenty pounds gosh. Gran sa is this wise but croker only wink. He sa slickest thing he ever done and have BEER in spotted dog.

Sept. 18.

Find farm dog who gaze at weedy calendar viz:

> If mistress haf a walk for me
> A model doggy i will be.

Throw stone for dog but he only take refuge under cow. i wash my hands of him.

Sept. 19.

a.r.p. come for traler as they think there fire on somewere.

Sept. 22.

Grate day viz gran throw down force spoon at brekfast and give stiring message Plough for victory. mr croker sa dang from state of market he will jolly well haf to but no plough. Gran sa Fidledee dee, make one. Cheers cheers all infeck-ted with enthusiasm mrs croker scrub dairy, gran croker knit furously and mr croker borow small plough from over to copleys place. Cheers cheers enter gran on tractor and zoom around field. Birds sing cows graze and chikens peck everbode. Read wizard story 9 chinese Murders to farm dog which promptly catch rat.

Sept. 23.
All in bed with colds. That is life.

All in bed with colds. That is life.

Sept. 24.
Moo.

Punch, 9 December 1942

MOLESWORTH OR LITTLE BY LITTLE

Contains: Diary of cads, big bullys, kanes, new masters, grandmothers and other bits of gen.

Oct. 18.

Arive back late in term after weedy harvesting it is top-hole to be back at good old st. cypranes again i don't think. molesworth 2 haf low morale viz blub bitterly against ropes in jim. propergander i sa skool days are happiest in life and he repli if this happiness give him stalingrad every time. Chiz fotherington-tomas comfort molesworth 2 with wizard sweets. Dercid to blub loudly but only get conduc mark (animal crys) fuste of the season. Tell jenkins but he sa shut up swanking he haf already 10 i.e. slack, yorning in chapel, stink bombs in prep and bad maners (7). Small but prickly thistle in matrons bed and so to innercent sleep.

Oct. 19.

Morning bell viz all boys leap from bed at thort of breakfast cheers cheers squadrons of sossages take off from plates and spoons zoom mightily MASTERS sneke in guiltily with yelow faces. Carry out begning of term inspecktion skool dog new bugs skool pig and dirty dick gardners boy all O.K. Test skool dog with trial conker which land in target area but am disgusted to find NEW MASTER who regard me venormously. He sa Hi you what your name: when i say molesworth 1 he sa Har! i haf heard of you. Tremble tremble try old wheeze i.e. look ashamed but no go get 3 conduc marks and when i say gosh 3 sir that a bit stiff he smirk and sa since i not satisfied he will give 4. This is skool record so thank him perlitely and ooze off to chass new bugs.

Oct. 20.

4 gosh i mean to say gosh chiz.

Oct. 24.

Pla touogh footer blues v whites and new master pla he wear red shirt v. girlie chiz he shout get it out to wing peason when peason get ball which is always as he best player. I pla strong but cool game at right back and hack everbode inkluding new master touogh touogh am human goriller. Unfortunately molesworth 2 drible round me chiz and am so disturbed i take pot shot into own goal as fotherington-tomas sulk becos he not captain. Cheers cheers new master too exorsted to make coments or adminster blip. BEER?

Oct. 25.

Canot get over molesworth 2 dribling round me.

Oct. 28.

More chizzes. Get bored with geog prep (italy) and add new patent touches draw 1000000 bombs very beatiful also mussolini the jackal who shake hands with new master. Gosh shadow fall on paper bones freeze behind me is new master who say Har got you and deliver weedy bonk with daily express. He sa pikture show remarkable talent who is man who shake hands with fasscist diktator. i repli another tyrant with a face like a nanny gote and get touogh blitzing chiz. molesworth 2 highly delited he shout go it sir chitty bang bang he is a fule.

Oct. 30.

Start to write wizard book Kanes and Tweeks i haf Felt by n. molesworth.

Oct. 31.

Get down to chap. 1 (sorts of kanes twitchy swishy bendy dog-headed etc) when fotherington-tomas come up he sa i am sorry you haf been in such hot water molesworth 1 old man would a conker that is conkerer of 43 be of any use? i repli absolutely none old horse buzz off but chiz as he press BOOK into my unwashed hand. Read it he sa it may bring comfort and skip weedily to give crumbs to ajacent birds. Look at book viz eric or little by little but no germans g. men spies, touoghs or flying forteresses ect chiz. Spend quiet half hol scrapping with peason also mob juniors who sing cristopfer robin at buckingham palace which molesworth 2 conduc he is an absolute swankpot. Recive wizard bruise on knee and do famous limping.

Nov. 3.

Still canot think how molesworth 2 got round me at footer.

Nov. 5.

Guy Forkes day. Old englishe festival. BONK.

Nov. 7.
Weedy french viz papa rat now in pritty pickle in the wood-shed it seem he will haf to turn and fight it out cheers cheers but chiz sentence 6 puss fall in well. deaf master roar with larfter very funny i must sa. Find BOOK eric or little by little in desk and cunningly read several chapters not bad.

Nov. 9.
Finish BOOK am deeply impressed.

Nov. 12. Purchase cheap rat from dirty dick gardners boy very fine specmen. peason advise new masters bed and molesworth 2 sa how about eating it but do not think. Dercid on good aktion viz give rat to skool dog he won't get one anyhow else but chiz as skool dog zoom off with rat to mr trimp (headmasters) study. Tremble tremble all boys to asemble in big skool who is culpritt who haf pute rat in coal skuttle? Prepare to look innercent but rember eric and zoom to feet. Sir sir it is i who haf played cruel jape. All boys are amazed viz peason fall backwards and molesworth 2 sa coo golly. Get 6 not worth it really. Good deed write to gran and describe nature.

Nov. 14.
i think i must haf slipped just as molesworth 2 approched with ball.

Nov. 15.

Grate day as mr pankhurst who was master at st. cypranes come back as flight leiutenant (r.a.f.) all boys sa gosh look and ask feeble questions viz. how many haf you shot down sir?

mr pankhurst come back as flight leiutenant

mr pankhurst sa about 10 but chiz as molesworth 2 shout sez you and zoom away he is feeble and think he finest pilot in the world becos he shoot down chikens, rooks and skool dog ect. jenkins sa Hope you will come back after war sir but me pankhurst sa no jolly fear and dig matron in ribs. New master sa 10 very impressive total for oficer in stores branch. Can he be jealous?

Nov. 17.

Read eric agane and confess to matron about thistle. Recive conduc mark which too light a punishment for sin i haf commited.

Nov. 18.

Peason sa Whats up all this confessing it is feeble. i repli peason peason you haf not yet read eric take the volume it will give you comfort. Do touogh writing viz chap 2 (bending over) but chiz as peason come up he confess he haf pinched 6 mars bars from my locker last year. Gosh i mean to sa. All boys now read BOOK and when mr trimp sa Who haf pute footer boots on skool pig whole skool confess chiz they are copy cats. mr trimp grately upset.

Nov. 19.

Gran arive at skool as she haf been deeply disturbed by my letter about nature she think i am ill. Grate event folows as new master zoom up in a bate he think i am buying fruit from applewoman (gran). Gran highly delited at prospekt of row with somebody. She sa Har are you not the son of my old butler who pinch the sherry go away you nasty little boy. New master retire with tale between legs gosh what a story. Fight all night not to tell peason.

Nov. 20.

10 out of 10 v.g. much better for geog from new master. Significant?

Nov. 22.

Give molesworth 2 BOOK to read as he haf large bag of sweets. He sa not bad but he prefer all about love also eat all sweets. What is the use? Thro book at molesworth 2 hit deaf master and zoom away to skool pig. Boo to eric and everbode else.

Nov. 23.

i must haf taken eye off ball.

As any
fule kno